More in this series:

The mafia, a smuggling ring and the wilds of Alaska are no match for this special operative. But a brazen redhead might be.

Elias Gasper's known as the do-it-all guy. From HALO jumps to calming hostages, he's on it. When he stumbles across a woman in hiding, he meets a new challenge in getting her to talk. While he's willing to add breaking through her silence to his list of skills, fighting his attraction still needs work.

Ruby Ryan is an alias, but doing anything it takes to save herself is real. She's used to switching sides, so cozying up to a hunky military man proves easy...maybe a little too easy. Not only are his kisses irresistible, but he has a way of making her laugh—something she hasn't done in a long time.

Gasper's abilities are tested even more when he must choose between helping his team and saving the strong woman with a hidden sweet side. His motto of "quitters never win" is his driving force, because for this mission, he's going to defend his teammates as well as the woman he'd give his life for.

XTREME MEASURES

BY

Em Petrova

Chapter One

"Let's play a game of which challenge do you choose? Not taking a breath for two minutes on a dive in the icy Bering Sea or hiking twenty miles through the Alaskan wilderness carrying a full load?"

Special Operative Elias Gasper pinned his captain with an are-you-screwing-with-me stare. "That's easy. I'd take the two minutes."

"And risk hypothermia?" His captain arched a brow.

"Damn right. I've been on enough hikes through these mountains with hunger pains gnawing at my stomach. At least after a dive in the cold sea, I can take a breath *and* have dinner."

The banter between Gasper and his captain cut off as they reached what appeared to be little more than a metal shack. On missions, he'd seen more than one pile of scrap passing as a structure in Alaska, and this one was no different—rust-streaked walls with paint flaking off and a roof that appeared to be patched in several spots.

They'd find the same things they had in the past—drugs, girls or both. Whatever it was, he was ready. Gasper's training had landed him here at the top of his game. Earning a position on the Xtreme Ops team had been the high point of his career.

"You know, regardless of what people think"—his breathing remained even as they ran through thick trees to the front of the building—"Alaska's as primitive as the Wild West was back in the day. Too many men, too many weapons and too few law enforcement officers."

"Don't forget whiskey. We all deserve a shot after this," his captain Penn Sullivan said into the comms unit. He skidded to a stop and waved in a series of gestures that would send the team to surround the exits. He flicked two fingers toward Gasper, indicating he was with him.

He gave a single nod of understanding. Then Penn ticked down on his fingers. *Three...two...go.*

Gasper lifted his rifle and fired clean through the lock. The report echoed through the metal structure, so when he and Penn ran in, weapons up, two men were already waiting for them.

A bullet whizzed past Gasper's ear. He looked the shooter dead in the eyes and returned the favor shot for shot. Only Gasper didn't miss. The man was thrown backward, hitting the floor with legs sprawled.

Penn dealt with the second guard in record time, and they moved into the building, swinging their weapons left and right. Shouts sounded in Russian.

Shit. He and Penn traded a glance. Just as they thought. The Bratva—the Russian mafia—was back in Alaska. Their presence was so insidious, the Xtreme Ops team had never completely driven them out the first few times.

Gasper translated the Russian in his mind, and Penn was fluent too. In his ear came Shadow's drawl. "Who keeps inviting these assholes? Captain, did you know we'd be dealing with the Russians again?"

"Negative."

Stopping this group was like sticking a finger over a water leak—it always popped up in another place. No matter how many times Homeland Security's Operation Freedom Flag sent their team to eradicate the crime group, they always showed their faces again.

In his head, he translated several conversations going on at once. When he heard the word "ship," he opened his mouth to speak to Penn. The explosion of a round of fire had him flattened on the floor. A hailstorm of bullets ricocheted around the big open room, and Gasper spotted two other team members pinned down.

Soldier-crawling on his belly, arm over arm, he attempted to move into a position where he could take out those guns. Right ahead of him, his captain crawled so fast that Gasper had to turn up the speed if he planned to guard his six. He wasn't about to let his team down.

"Anything goes!" Penn shouted to the team. Meaning if they didn't take a single survivor out of here to hold prisoner, then these motherfuckers asked for it.

Two of his teammates popped out of nowhere, spraying bullets over the shooters. One fell. Another dropped with a scream of pain.

So did Pax.

Gasper watched his teammate crumple, his leg shot out from underneath him.

"Son of a bitch!"

Penn, safe for the moment, took his eyes off the threat long enough to see what had Gasper bellowing.

"Go, go, go!" He waved for Gasper to reach their fallen brother.

He scrambled, slithering across the gap. The breeze off a round of bullets fluttered the cloth of his pants. *Too damn close for comfort.*

Doing a tuck and roll, he pitched up beside Pax. Through his face paint, the man was sweating. Hands clasped around his shin, he met Gasper's stare.

"I got you, bro. Hang on." He whipped out some cloth and knotted it around the worst of Pax's wrecked lower leg. Pax didn't make a sound, but his face grew paler, and sweat poured off him.

"We'll cover you, Jack! Move him out!" Penn's order flooded into Gasper's ear and hit his brain. His

4

nickname of Jack, for jack-of-all-trades, spurred him to action.

"I'm gonna throw you over my shoulders. It's gonna hurt."

"Hurt you or me?" Though Paxton joked, he looked about to throw up, pass out or…

Gasper didn't want to think about what the other possibility might be. He positioned himself for a fireman's carry, gripping Pax's right arm and leg, and then stood so his body draped across his shoulders.

As he whirled, several bullets meant for his skull slammed into the wall in front of him.

"Fucking hell." Pax's voice expelled as a groan.

He was losing a lot of blood. He may lose his leg. Gasper had to move him the hell out—now.

"Gasper to Helo," he called to their chopper pilot Cora.

"10-4, Gasper."

"I'm on my way out with Pax. He's hit."

A pause sounded on her end, and then her voice came steady and clear. "I got him covered."

As Gasper burst out of the building, the pops of gunfire faded. He ate up the ground, hauling slightly more weight than his full pack that Penn had been bantering with him about just minutes before. Paxton weighed a good two-twenty's worth of pure muscle.

As he ran, Cora pummeled him for information about Pax's injuries, his current status and ETA to the waiting chopper. Gasper answered them all, breath coming in spurts as he ran for both of them.

Cora sounded concerned, but that didn't mean the situation would end badly. Paxton and Cora had graduated from their special forces training together. As far as teammates went, they were tight, and her pause when Gasper told her who was hit told him the woman had taken a moment to compose herself.

Could be worse for her, though. Her husband and their fearless captain, Penn, could have been hit.

Paxton's body suddenly went slack, and he realized the man had passed out. The pain of being jostled had probably proved too much for him. At least Gasper didn't have to worry about hurting him more as he sprinted with all his speed through the trees.

His boot caught a root, and he almost went down, but he managed to find his footing and burst into the clearing half a mile away. The chopper sat in the darkness, a hulking beast made of metal and blades.

The person standing at the chopper spun toward them, weapon ready. Through darkness, he couldn't make out her face, but the set of her shoulders revealed it was Cora, and she was relieved to see them. She slipped her weapon along her spine and ran to meet them.

"He's unconscious." Gasper grunted as he dropped to his knees and lowered Paxton to the ground.

Cora was already in first-aid mode, checking the man's pulse and respirations. Then she glanced at the blood soaking his camo, inky black in the night. "Help me put him on the chopper. I'll stabilize him there."

He picked up his brother, this time slinging him onto his back, and carried him the few feet to the silent chopper.

Cora knelt beside Paxton. "Go, Gasper. I got this."

"You sure?" If something went south and the man started to code, Cora would be left alone to save his life.

"Yes! Go! Our team needs you!" She was already at work, cutting off Paxton's pantleg and assessing the damage, which, to Gasper, appeared to be pretty damn catastrophic.

He took off for the trees, though, and minutes later made it out the other side. For a crushing heartbeat, he noted the silence hanging over the building the Russian mafia had been operating out of.

"Where the hell are you guys?" he asked his team.

The words were cut off by all hell breaking loose. Shots and screams. The stench of fire fueled by oil.

Never quit. Slow down when you're dead.

He rushed inside and picked up where he left off. Paxton and Broshears had been teamed up, but Broshears and the captain were now partnered. When Gasper joined them, Penn eyed him.

"Nice to see you, Jack."

"What's goin' on?" he asked as if they weren't pinned down in a deadly turf war.

A wall separated them from the main space, but from what he saw, two men lay dead on the floor.

"Lip's sharpshooting is winning the day. He's got the advantage and has taken out half a dozen men. Shadow, Beckett and Winston are cut off from us, though. Over there." He pointed. "They found the women."

"There's always women," Gasper said.

Broshears snorted in response. Although the Bratva preferred drugs and women as their main trade, the Xtreme Ops team had seen a lot more crimes from them. The war in Alaska would definitely be hard-won, and this was but one more battle.

Broshears and Gasper took orders from their captain's silent commands. They got into position, prepared to end this.

Then Cora's voice came into their ears. Penn's head snapped up, and for a moment, he didn't move.

"I've got to evacuate Paxton. He's on the downslide. Lifting him out is his only chance."

Penn's throat moved in a long swallow. He gritted out, "Go. We'll find our way to safety and rendezvous with you later."

8

After Cora ended the communication, determination broke over his captain's face. "Let's end this, Xtreme Ops. For Pax."

Ruby Ryan twitched aside the dark green curtain, sewn by her grandmother's own gnarled, arthritic hands decades ago, and peeked outside.

White Fog, Alaska, population 202, looked the same as it had the day before. And the day before that too. The town clinging to the Alaskan coast boasted a gas station with inflated prices, a convenience store, a laundromat, and B&B with a cranky owner past his prime.

And one bar/restaurant/hostel. At least that was how Ruby's Place appeared on the surface to anyone happening to wander into White Fog. They came to photograph the mountains and seals basking on the rocky shores in the sun, and they left because the people of White Fog were pretty damn unfriendly. They stuck to themselves.

And nobody did that more than Ruby.

Today she wished for once that she could sleep in, rather than wake up to see to the bar and restaurant and check on the girls who worked here and lived on the upper floor.

A few thumps and bumps coming from above told her some of them were awake. Some probably never went to bed—their gentleman callers saw to that. Hostel…brothel…what was a few letters' difference?

She pushed out a sigh and surveyed her small quarters off the kitchen. She always hated this place growing up when her grandmother, the original Ruby, owned it. Now that duty invaded each and every corner of her life, she despised it more.

But those duties called, and she had to walk out there with a smile slapped on her face and endure it for another day.

It was harder this time of year. Some folks around here told rumors that she suffered from seasonal depression, but she knew the real cause to be much darker than that.

She pulled on stretchy black pants and a long-sleeve white top that hung off her shoulder to reveal skin freckled by the barest hint of the Alaskan sun. Then she wandered into the bathroom to tame her wild red hair.

Peering at her reflection always made her sigh. Each day that passed, she saw more of her grandmother in her face, which meant she was fading, right? What beauty she had wasted on slinging food to ungrateful staff and customers, sustained on caffeine and the occasional decadent bite of chocolate bar she snuck on her break.

And dealing with *the guys* only added to the dead expression behind her eyes. Her bouncers.

Too many layers went into Ruby's Place, many buried so deep beneath the foundation that even ghosts couldn't burrow down to find them. The bouncers preferred it that way, and she was tasked to keep it as such.

If anything slipped through... Well, she had a lot of reasons not to let that happen.

After scrubbing her face so it was shiny and using eye drops to cut the redness that always seemed to be there from lack of sleep, she went out of her room and made certain to lock it behind her. The last thing she needed was a strange man in her bed, and so many were coming and going at all times that she couldn't take the risk one might wander into her room.

Out front, the glow of the few lights she kept on over the bar looked green against the glass liquor bottles. She walked over to the breaker panel and flipped a switch to light up the entire bar area as well as the restaurant.

More bumps sounded above her, and seconds later, a man lurched down the stairs, half tumbling in his drunkenness, with her girl Abby right behind him. Abby was one of the few girls who spoke English.

The man stumbled to his feet and staggered against the wall.

"What the hell's going on?" Ruby reached for her baseball bat. "Is he giving you trouble, Abby?"

"He pissed in my bed. The disgusting, filthy hog!"

11

Ruby stepped up to the customer who Abby had entertained of her own free will. All the girls got to pick, and if they said no, then Ruby enforced their decision. Ruby didn't force them to work here — other people did that — and the least she could do was take care of them.

She held the wooden bat an inch from the man's face. "You got cash on you?"

He blinked and finally nodded.

"You just bought yourself a soiled mattress. Put what money you have on the bar and get the hell outta here!"

He took a single glance at Ruby's face and saw she was as serious as the beat-down she'd give him if he didn't comply. Not to mention the bouncers who were coming out of the woodwork to stand on either side of the exit.

The customer dug through his wrinkled clothes until he located his pockets. A bunch of bills hit the bar top, and Ruby gave him a satisfied nod. "Get out." She twitched her head toward the exit.

When the man didn't move fast enough, the bouncers came forward to assist him on his way. Both were huge, muscled, with shaved heads and a ton of Russian tattoos.

Mafia tattoos.

Ruby turned away from the scene and tipped her head to peer up the stairs at Abby. "You okay other than the mattress?"

"Yes." She set her stubborn jaw.

"Get cleaned up and dressed. I'll have the guys carry your mattress out and we'll find you a new one."

"Thank you, Ruby. You always have our backs."

Until the day she couldn't stand it another minute and she took off.

She examined the girl, whose vitality was fading fast too. When Abby had come to White Fog, she was in the blush of youth, with blue eyes and waist-length thick brown hair bearing a healthy glow. She learned English quicker than most girls who arrived, and her accent had fled the fastest.

But men such as the last customer had placed a hard knife edge in those blue eyes and her hair hung more lifeless every day as her unhealthy lifestyle took over. But the girls never did drugs — that was Ruby's single, solid, hold-fast rule. If she found out they did, she no longer had a room for them.

Too much to deal with before her first coffee of the day. Plus, the bouncers were looking at her expectantly. She could almost hear their stomachs rumbling for breakfast.

"Abby, find Jenicka. She's cooking today."

Abby nodded before disappearing from the top of the stairs. Ruby turned to the bar. Too often, she was tempted to drink away her cares with one of the twenty bottles there. But all she still had left of her

13

sanity was her ability to think straight, so she went for the coffee in the kitchen instead.

When she heard the bouncers talking in the low rumble of their native Russian she couldn't stand listening to, she switched on a transistor radio and drowned them out in old pop music.

She barely had two sips of coffee in her before one of the bouncers, Maxim, poked his head in. He went by Max on US soil, as if anyone would ever mistake him for anything but the overgrown badass Russian he was.

"You forgot to put the menu up in the window, Ruby."

Her stomach cramped. God, how had she gotten distracted enough by a soiled mattress to forget that part of her job?

"I'm coming."

She gathered the menu placards she taped in the glass of the front door each day. What day was it? Friday? Saturday? It was easy to lose track in this place, but it mattered what day it was.

Shipments came in on Fridays.

It was definitely Friday.

With her stomach churning now, she carried the menu and tape to the front of the restaurant and carefully taped the menus to face out on the right side of the glass. Right was coming, left going. It made a massive difference.

With her job complete, she stepped away. After she gave the signal, it wouldn't be long before she expected the truck to arrive.

"Keep it cool, Ruby," Max said.

She turned for the kitchen. "Gonna finish my coffee."

As soon as she reached the kitchen, though, she leaned against the counter, breathing hard. All it would take was a single slip and her whole world would come crashing down on her. She'd be arrested for crimes she was watching be committed but she wasn't truly taking part in.

And the men who held her father could decide that she wasn't working off his debt fast enough, and things would go up in flames.

"Ruby." This time the other bouncer, Mikhail, who the girls called Big Mike, entered her sanctuary and broke through what peace she'd tried to scrape up for herself.

She threw him a glare.

"You know what you have to do."

She set a hand on her hip. "Shouldn't it at least look like you work for me?" She slammed her mug down on the counter and rushed past Big Mike to the front even as he went to the rear to allow another kind of shipment in.

Ruby's heart wouldn't stop racing until late tonight, after it was all over.

Through the glass on the door, she could see people decked out in fishing gear reading the menu.

She opened the door for them. They kept their heads down as they filed in, their slickers with their hoods up disguising them as fishermen just coming in off the water with their shipments of crab to sell.

Four of them walked by her, and then five. She peered out. "That's all?" she asked Max, who watched them enter.

He gave her a nod. Sometimes there were upward of a dozen "fishermen" entering Ruby's Place.

The newcomers stood in the middle of the room, waiting for her to give them the next command.

Holding her head high, she said in some of the crude Russian she'd learned over the past year in this business, "Come with me," and led them into the kitchen. As she entered, she heard the telltale click of the back door, where the rest of the shipment had been delivered. The scent of the wood barrels of "beer" filled her stomach with dread, but she worked through it and took charge. There was much to do.

She held open a door off the kitchen, and the five fishermen entered. "Take off your gear," she said in clear Russian. "Stow your garments in here." She pointed to a large wooden trunk that would be locked up and loaded onto a ship headed to Russia to be reused.

Piece by piece, the raingear, hoods and thick pants that concealed womanly curves were stripped

16

off until five young, frightened women who didn't know what was coming to them stood before her.

"Welcome. I'm Ruby, and I'll tell you the rules."

Ruby glanced from face to face and though she didn't show it, her shoulders wanted to droop. Most of these girls hadn't yet lost hope in the false promise they'd been brought to America under.

They still believed, and that crushed her spirit most of all.

Half a dozen men sat in a row with their backs to the wall, their wrists and ankles bound. Several bore the tattoos of monasteries and cathedrals on the backs of their hands as well as any other exposed skin. Also, Gasper noticed a few thieves' stars, which were important status symbols in prison.

And every man had a glare of hatred for the Xtreme Ops team.

Penn paced before them, interrogating them in Russian. All his questions went unanswered, though a man on the end dropped his head.

Gasper flicked his jaw to Broshears, who stood closest. When Broshears tipped his head to hear what he had to say, Gasper pointed. "That's our man. He's the one who will talk in the end."

Broshears eyed Gasper. "Penn thinks there are a lot more women they got out when we burst in. We don't have much time to stop them. You're the member of this team who talks down the hostages and everybody in between. Maybe you should speak to him."

"Not yet. Penn's breaking them down, I can see it."

Just then, Penn jerked his head up and gestured to the team to each take a man.

Gasper strode forward and grabbed the first guy by the wrist bonds, pulling him to a stand. "Follow me," he said in the distinctive accent of Ukraine.

He hauled the man across the room to a chair and pushed him into it. The number of cupolas on the cathedral of the Russian's tattoo indicated the times he'd been to prison for stealing.

"Four times, eh?" he switched to English just to see if the man indicated he understood. In his experience, foreigners typically spoke fluent English but pretended otherwise, especially during questioning.

His eyes shifted to Gasper's face, and he didn't look away. Neither did Gasper.

"Where are the drugs going after you deliver them?" he asked.

The man remained silent, eyes roaming over Gasper as if picking out his vulnerable spots. But he already knew the Russian's — the eyes, throat, stomach and balls. Hit any of those, and the man would double over, screaming.

He continued to try to pump information from the man, and around them, the Xtreme Ops team did the same to the rest of the Russians. No one was getting anywhere.

One Russian man sporting a bald head spat a glob of mucus at Lipton.

"Oh shit," he said under his breath just as Lipton leaped forward and grabbed the Russian by the throat. He shook him, screaming obscenities in Russian, English and…

"Is that Latvian?" Hepburn, called Shadow, drawled in question.

"If you don't answer me, you'll regret it. Comply now and you might only be shipped home," Penn barked at another.

Gasper switched his attention from the man sitting in front of him and again latched his focus on the man at the end, who Broshears was firing questions at.

They weren't going to learn jack shit from these guys unless they tried a different tactic. And while Lipton had released his prisoner and cooled off a measure, this wasn't what the Xtreme Ops team stood for. They were elite.

Leaving his prisoner, Gasper walked over to Penn. His captain turned his head aside to hear what he had to say.

"Let me at that one. I can make him talk," he murmured.

Penn side-eyed him. "You sure about that, Special Operative? I don't think they'd talk if they were waterboarded."

"Somethin' about that guy — hell, he's still a kid — makes me think I can squeeze more from him. And I'll need a map."

Penn didn't indicate any surprise when he nodded. "Broshears, swap with Gasper."

Broshears stood to switch prisoners.

"Sullivan!" Penn called out.

Cora stood across the room from Penn. She'd medevacked Paxton to the nearest hospital with a trauma unit and hurried back to the rest of the team, but she still appeared shaken.

She snapped to attention at her husband calling her by their shared last name.

"Gasper needs a map."

She nodded.

When Gasper drew the kid to his feet and led him in baby steps, because of his bound feet, across the room to a table, he pointed to the chair. The kid dropped into it and set his elbows on the surface, his ink on full display. For a person so young, he was deep in the mafia life.

They sat assessing each other until a minute later, when Cora approached with a map. She spread it on the table and stood back, arms crossed, watching.

Gasper crooked his finger at her to come closer. She did, bracing a hand on the table to lean in.

"Where do you think the drugs were supposed to go?" he asked Cora in Russian so the prisoner couldn't claim not to understand.

She studied the map of Alaska for a minute. Tracing a finger along the path of a well-known route in the drug trade, she ended on a small city.

Gasper noted her movement from the corner of his eye—his attention was on the prisoner. "There's plenty of smuggling going on in the north, though. They could be headed to a small commercial fishing town. They'd retrieve more per gram up here." Gasper pointed to a location on the map but tracked the prisoner's eyes.

He stared at the map but didn't move while Gasper and Cora talked over the situation and made guesses.

Then Gasper caught the kid's eyes slanting to the south of Alaska.

Cora stilled. She'd seen it too.

To make sure, Gasper continued the conversation, discussing shipments the DEA regularly intercepted. Again, the kid glanced at the south and then away.

"Captain, a word please," Gasper called out.

Penn stopped midsentence in his questioning and strode over. Gasper met him in the center of the room to have a private word.

"My prisoner's indicated twice that the shipment could be going south."

"Anchorage?"

21

"Possibly. I'll continue to drill him, but I doubt any of them will give us a town name. I'll draw a circle around the region of the map that his eyes went to and start digging from there. The guys can raise the question of Anchorage and everywhere within a hundred miles and see if any of the prisoners crack."

"I doubt they fucking will," Penn growled. "They're tough motherfuckers."

"How many runs would you guess they're making a month?" Gasper asked.

"Hard to say. Ships are fast; they're probably hitting our shores with shipments several times a month. I'll get with the DEA in Anchorage and see what they know."

"I'm sure they're bringing more than heroin on those ships. We know what these assholes are typically trading."

Penn exchanged a look with Gasper that told him he was right. "Take the map, and you and Cora form a plan to search that area. We'll drop these assholes into the hands of the FBI and then head out."

"Yes, sir." Gasper pivoted, but Penn stopped him with a wave of his hand.

"Good job, Jack. We'll add reading body language to your list of skills."

He was always humbled when his brothers referred to him as the jack-of-all-trades. He didn't nearly deserve such deference to his skills when they all had plenty between them.

He responded with a dip of his head. Before Penn turned away, he said, "Captain?"

Penn gave him his attention.

"What did that guy say to Lipton to heat him up?"

"He said he will have his friends hunt down Lip's family."

"Goddamn."

"It's no wonder he reacted. I can't say I wouldn't do the same." With a glance at Cora, Penn took off across the room again.

As soon as Gasper and Cora were alone with the map spread between them, he felt the woman relax.

"You good?" he asked.

She sighed. "Something about these guys has me a little freaked out."

He examined her. "It takes a lot to shake you. You've survived two plane crashes, for God's sake."

"I can't put my finger on the reason. It's like they're all joined in silence because they know something else is coming."

Gasper grinned. "I think we can officially call you a special operative now, Cora. Your gut instincts have kicked in."

"Do they accompany a sense of doom and feeling as if you're walking into a trap?" she quipped in return.

"That's the one."

"And here I thought that taco ration didn't sit well with me."

His laugh further broke the tension, and both of them relaxed enough to turn their focus to the map. He grabbed two pens and withdrew a shoelace from his pocket.

"You're more prepared than the others," Cora said.

He grunted. "Never know when a little bit of string will come in handy. Like this." He tied it around both pens, set one upright over Anchorage and drew a circle around the area with the string to guide the other pen in a makeshift compass.

Cora stood back, eyes fastened on the map. "To the north, we've got some trails and wilderness. East is Prince William Sound."

"A good port to ship from."

"I'm wondering about this." He tapped Moose Pass, Alaska, to the south. "We already know a lot of drugs trickle down through small towns to bigger ones. And there isn't a hell of a lot to do there, which is when people start getting creative."

"Such as speedballs of coke and heroin?"

"Exactly. Problem is, this is a lot of ground for us to cover. We know where the drugs are coming in, and approximately where they could be going, but it's going to take a while to put a stop to it."

"My concern is with their other trade. Where are the girls ending up?"

"Good point—check into all the previous busts for trafficking we've seen over the past year, and we'll start there. And it's a good idea to dig deeper, find some brothels." They'd located several barrels containing drugs from that bunker and managed to win three women out of the deal too.

"Those will be more difficult. It's not as if we're Vegas."

"We might still wring some intel from the Russians." Gasper listened for sounds of raised voices but heard nothing. All yelling had come to a halt, and Lipton must have regained his temper.

"Doubt it." Cora brushed a strand of blonde hair off her forehead. "But you found us a place to start. Guess that's why we call you jack-of-all-trades—you keep on surprising us with your skills."

Chapter Two

Ruby's grandmother always told her that working in low light would ruin her eyes. But here she was, hunched over the desk at two in the morning, poring over the books.

Five new girls meant five new mouths to feed. Sixteen girls total.

Too many to justify not letting a few go.

Her guts churned. She didn't have any responsibility to them once they walked out, but the only other placement for them in this country left her veins iced over with dread. Not a single girl under her roof deserved that fate.

It was bad enough they were selling their bodies right over her head. Her grandmother would roll in her grave if she could see what had become of her bar.

The scratch of pencil on paper was the only sound in the room as Ruby ran through the numbers over and over. Though it was unlikely, she had to try to unearth an extra zero that would keep her girls here with her a little longer. But doing so meant she'd have the impossible task of soothing the Russian mafia. The group also known as the Bratva wanted to push the girls through her establishment a lot faster, but lately Ruby had been trying to slow that process.

Their rule said no more than ten girls could remain under her roof at once. As of yesterday, she had eleven. The girls would be taken away, and she'd never know what happened to them or if they were happy...

Of course they weren't happy. Who the hell was in this world? The black weight of despair smothered her, and she sat back, rubbing her eyes.

When the heavy footstep sounded at her threshold, she dropped her hands and glared at Max, but that didn't deter the man from taking a seat in the chair across from her.

She sighed and picked up her pencil again. Having the men breathing down her neck at all hours of the day was bad enough, but seeing the pistol tucked into Max's waistband in plain sight had her even more on edge.

Plus, he liked to leer at her. Lately she'd taken to sleeping with a knife under her pillow and a chair stuffed against the handle of her locked bedroom door. Between the bouncers and the men entertained upstairs, she couldn't be too careful.

Shooting a glance at the cold, hard steel cradled against Max's body made her hand slip on the pencil. What would it take for him to shoot her? Or worse, the man she was doing this all for—her father?

She gulped down her fear and forced her breathing to calm. Outthinking Max or Big Mike wasn't difficult—it was outwitting the men who gave them orders that was dangerous.

"Have you finished recording the new shipment yet?" he asked her.

She didn't glance up. "Yes. It hasn't all dropped yet."

He twitched his hand in a manner that drew her attention to the movement. Her heart thundered. It would take one twitch and she'd be dead. That might be a blessing, honestly, but she couldn't leave her father out in the cold. He'd gotten them into this horrible situation, but dammit, she was smart enough to get them both out. She had to be—she just hadn't figured out how to do it yet.

Also, there were the girls. Sixteen of them now, all speaking little to no English and new to the US, without visas or any hope of making their way besides on their backs with their legs spread.

That black kernel of fear that had long ago been planted deep in Ruby's soul sprouted roots. Sometimes she could hack down the thick, woody stem of the terror and bury it beneath the soil. But other times, it seemed to sink its roots deeper, and tonight, it was a damn beanstalk.

She narrowed her eyes on Max. "Don't you ever sleep?"

He cocked a thick, furry brow. "Don't you? Tell me about the shipment. What is missing?"

She swallowed hard. "Three girls," she said quietly.

He stiffened. "Three?"

"And several barrels."

He reached to his side, and she braced herself for impact of a bullet between the eyes, but a second later, he had his phone in hand. Relief spread a thick layer of nausea through her stomach.

When someone on the other end of the line answered, Max shifted to his feet, extending to his full height. In the low ceiling of her office, she always expected his head to bump the plaster.

In rapid Russian, he conversed with the person. She understood every single word and wished to hell she was ignorant of what she'd suspected had happened and now *knew* had.

Max ended the call with a grunt and lowered the phone to pierce her in his heavy stare. "Some of the shipment was intercepted."

Her insides roiled. "How?"

"At the stop-off. An invasion of the warehouse." He spoke the word *warehouse* using a *V* instead of a *W*.

She arched a brow. "What happens now?"

He shrugged, as if having some girls and drugs confiscated and now gone missing was of no consequence to him. But she was held responsible,

29

even though most of the transactions were beyond her control.

She stood and faced Max. "We can't afford to be sloppy. Your men aren't doing their jobs, and I'm the one who will pay."

Wordlessly, he held out his phone. She winced at what she knew she'd see there — the live-cam feed of her father in that room. Tied up, beaten. His eyes swollen shut. His hours were counting down. How much longer did he have before his captors made the call to end his life?

"Look at it!" Max commanded.

She directed her stare to the phone screen. She might be seeing a caged animal who bore the same red hair she did, but she forced herself to disconnect or risk her own sanity.

"I'll figure something out. I'll ask those five girls who did come in what happened."

Max nodded, slightly mollified. He nodded toward the stack of menus on the corner of her desk. "Don't forget."

How could she forget to put the menu on display in the front door first thing in the morning? Half the night, she'd lie awake wishing she never had to tape the papers on the left side, and yet tomorrow, she would do exactly that.

Right meant coming. Left going.

In the morning, some of her girls would be leaving her, sold to the highest bidder. There was nothing she could do to stop that, or her father being beaten in his prison somewhere in Russia or her soul from being drained by the hour in this place.

What could she do but square her shoulders and face up to what her life had become?

"He made it out of surgery. It's gonna be a long road to recovery, but he's alive."

The team breathed a collective sigh of relief as Penn conveyed the news about Paxton.

Gasper's chest had been burning with worry for their fallen brother since the man passed out during that run through the dark forest. It didn't stop burning now, either.

Paxton may never return to duty.

His leg had been fucked the hell up. He was surprised the surgeons had managed to save it at all. The vision of the mangled mess of bone and flesh and blood had been haunting Gasper ever since he laid the man on the floor of the chopper.

"Can we do anything?" he asked Penn.

"There's nothing more we can do for Pax now. From here on, this is his battle."

They all sobered, thinking through their captain's statement. It hit too close to home for them all.

Penn grew silent for a moment, letting them all gather their thoughts. Then he swept the team with his sharp stare. "You're all aware of our reason for coming to Anchorage?"

Every man nodded. Gasper just hoped to hell he wasn't wrong in what he'd seen. That prisoner in the bunker had definitely glanced toward the part of the map, where Anchorage was located. He never double-checked his facts, because he didn't have to. He remembered everything. And he hadn't made a mistake about the man's body language either.

"We're splitting into teams to further this investigation. Any and all intel in this case will help us pin these motherfuckers to the ground and stop them. So make sure you're asking the right questions. Got it?" Penn met each man's gaze, gaining their agreement before giving orders. "State police — Lipton, Beckett and Broshears." Penn moved through the group. "DEA — Winston and Day, you're both with me. Anchorage PD — Shadow and Jack. Cora will remain here to provide backup as needed."

Gasper gave his captain a nod and turned to Shadow. The orders given, they headed straight out to tackle the city. With Anchorage being the biggest city within that circle he'd drawn on the map, higher-ups made the decision to start here. If the results of their investigation came up blank, they'd spread to the outlying areas of that circle.

Several vehicles sat in the parking lot for their use, and Shadow climbed behind the wheel. "I know you prefer to drive, but too damn bad," he drawled.

Gasper chuckled. "Shotgun beats being stuck in the back of that SUV we usually travel in. I've been carsick too many times to count."

Shadow cranked the engine. "Big strong guy like you gets carsick? I've been working with you a while now. How did I never know this?"

"Because I don't air my shortcomings. Neither do you."

"True enough." He waited for Lipton to pull out ahead of them before bumping out of the parking lot. "What do you think we'll learn from the Anchorage PD?"

"Hopefully, some lead to show us we're on the right track. If there are women and drugs moving through their city, they'll know."

"Can't keep track of everything."

"Good point. But shit this big doesn't go unnoticed. A group of Russian women being dumped off with no homes or jobs is a red flag to a lot of people that something's going on. Any of the guys willing to buy them are usually stupid too. One of them's bound to talk."

"You're right. And don't forget about the drugs."

"Right—black tar heroin is everywhere, but white is the purest form, and that's what we found on the Russians. That's gonna stick out. Word gets around fast in this place."

They'd performed enough missions that brought them through Anchorage that they were familiar with the darkest and dirtiest parts of the city.

"Do you have any idea what happened to the girls we found in that bunker?" Shadow didn't glance away from the road as he navigated the streets.

"Penn didn't say, and if he did, I didn't hear it. I'm sure they were taken into custody by the FBI, questioned and probably put back on a ship to Russia." Gasper had been deep in thought over the girls ever since they discovered them in a back room. When they blasted into the hidden room, three women had been huddling there, whispering.

"I can tell something is bugging you about those women. What vibration are you picking up?" Shadow asked.

Gasper shifted his shoulders in a shrug. "They stopped talking the minute we walked in."

"Could be scared."

"Could be hiding something."

"Like what?" Shadow asked.

"Like more women who got out before they could."

Shadow issued a low whistle. "Have you discussed this with Penn?"

"I told him my hunch, but until we do what we have to here, tracing any possible girls—who may not even exist—could be a wild goose chase." He pointed

34

to a side road. "Take this shortcut to the police department."

"This isn't a shortcut. You just want to swing by the barbecue place."

Gasper shot him a crooked grin.

"Ahhh, see? I knew it."

"No harm in us grabbing a real lunch before we get down to business. Don't tell me you're not sick of those taco MREs. There's not enough Tabasco in the world to make me eat another one. Besides, we won't waste time—there's a drive-thru."

"What is it with you and barbecue? I thought you grew up on lute…lute…what the fuck is it called again?"

Gasper chuckled. "Lutefisk. I did. And it's good. But I don't see a lutefisk joint anywhere around here, so I'll have to settle for barbecue."

"The way you describe that dish sounds disgusting, man. I'd rather sit down with a roasted rat than have fish soaked in lye."

"It's not for everyone, but if you grow up with something, it reminds you of who you are every time you eat it. What did you grow up eating, Hep?" He still wasn't totally accustomed to calling Hepburn by his recently earned nickname of Shadow. They'd been friends too long.

"Good ole Southern cookin'. Cornbread, for one. Love me some cornbread. Maybe the barbecue joint has some." He turned into the restaurant drive-thru, and the ladies who served their food through the delivery window shot them weird looks.

"You Air Force?" the girl asked.

"No," Shadow said flatly, without flirting as he once might have. Since he'd fallen in love with Sascha, he was a changed man. He took the bags of food and their drinks and drove away.

With a meal far better than a chicken or taco military ration in his stomach, Gasper felt more ready to tackle the challenges of talking to the Anchorage PD. Not every law enforcement office in the US was willing to work with them — too often they thought the Xtreme Ops team was stepping on their toes.

Minutes later they were seated with the two officers handling most of the drug cases in the area. They discussed what was running through the city and where they believed it came in, but neither man knew much about trafficked women. And they hadn't heard a murmur about any Russian women passing through the area.

Out of the corner of his eye, Gasper shot Shadow a look. This always happened. Either they didn't want to provide intel on a case they were currently working hard, or they'd just stopped giving a damn. In a state with more than its share of drug and alcohol abuse, people became desensitized pretty damn quick.

The officer leaned back in his chair, boot casually hitched over his knee as he eyed Gasper. "Give us the details on the case, and if we get wind of anything, we'll be in touch with you."

Gasper could see they were through here, so he stood. Shadow thanked the officers for speaking with them, but the minute they were outside, Shadow issued a low noise from his throat.

Swinging his head toward him, Gasper noted the frustration on his teammate's face. "Did you get the feeling those guys thought we were stepping on their toes?"

Shadow grunted. "Every damn minute we were in there. They cooperated, sure, but they don't understand why we're working a case like this."

"It sounds a little beneath us, if you break it into small chunks like drugs and trafficked women. But we've been fighting the Russian mafia since the day we landed in Alaska."

"Exactly. Get the captain on the line. Let's see what they found out from the DEA."

Gasper snorted. "Probably a whole lot less than we did."

But he was wrong. Once they all rallied in the parking lot again, they discovered that Penn's visit to the DEA had drummed up the name of a port city within the radius Gasper had drawn on the map.

"Lipton, whattaya got on that town?" Penn asked.

"White Fog, Alaska. Population around two hundred. Primary industry, fishing and tourism."

Gasper glanced at the screen Lipton held up for them all to see. The aerial map showed little more than what would be a truck stop in any other part of the country.

He studied the few buildings on the map. "I've taken dumps bigger than that town."

Several chuckles followed, but everyone was thinking the same thing—what better place to fly under the radar than a very small, inconsequential town with little more than a bar and restaurant and a few other businesses?

Gasper leaned over the screen and pointed to the map. "Well, boys, look on the bright side."

Penn gave a nod. "Fewer people to sift through."

Gasper scratched at his head. "I was thinking that at least there's a place to grab a beer."

Chapter Three

"Ruby, where do you want me to put this?" One of her girls had a bundle of dirty bedding in her arms.

Ruby wanted to snap like a mom at a kid who'd been taught long ago how to do a chore, but she bit her tongue. The girl was new. She didn't know all of Ruby's expectations yet.

She pointed to a room off the kitchen. "That's the laundry. We do our own clothes, bedding and towels around here," she told her.

The girl nodded and headed off to the laundry room, leaving Ruby to deal with another issue — the matter of the menu. With the pages spread out on the counter before her, she wished she could make the call about which window to tape them in today. Even though it wasn't Tuesday, when shipments usually went out, there were always men lurking around, just waiting to score a bride.

Or sex slave.

Her stomach churned at what she must do. Selling off a few girls was the only way — and the

39

Bratva wouldn't have any reservations in letting her know that.

Her father's image as she'd last seen him loomed in her mind. His blue-gray eyes that used to smile on her swollen shut.

Decision made, she grabbed the menu pages and the tape. The weather was mild today, which meant the bar and restaurant were illuminated by a warm glow that belied her feelings at what she must do in order to go on surviving.

She didn't want to think about those girls upstairs who would be sold off like cattle the minute she slapped the menu pages on the left.

Quickly, before she could have regrets and change her mind, she taped the menus up on the left side and rushed to the kitchen again. Two girls were in there helping out by preparing the midday meal. None of them ate breakfast — the girls were up all night with gentlemen callers and Ruby's stomach was always cramped too much to eat in the mornings.

The aroma of pasta sauce filled the kitchen — her grandmother's recipe. But she tried not to let her stomach turn at the scent. Her insides jittered, and bile pushed up her throat.

She broke for the trash can, leaning over it and retching.

"Oh, poor dove." A kitchen girl gathered her hair off her face. "Anushka, fetch her some water."

Ruby's stomach heaved, but nothing came up — there wasn't anything in there. Eyes watering, she dragged in a deep breath and tried to calm herself. She couldn't afford to lose her shit today, of all days.

Slowly, she straightened from the trash can. Anushka held out a glass of water, which she took with what she could muster for a weak smile. While she took small sips, the girls threw her glances.

Finally, Inessa, who'd been holding her hair, said what was on her mind. "Are you with child?"

Ruby nearly choked on the water. "No. I haven't been... No."

She couldn't recall the last time a man had been in her bed, and after dealing with her bouncers and a lot of other horrible men, she couldn't be further from inviting one in.

"If you are, Polina knows some herbs..." Inessa went on as if she didn't believe Ruby.

"I'm certain. I'm fine. Just a little queasy this morning. Must be something I ate last night." She put more effort into her smile to convince the girls, and eventually they drifted back to their duties, making pasta for lunch and a few other daily specials for the few townspeople who would drift in.

Ruby closed her eyes and steeled herself. Some of the girls would leave today. It wouldn't be long before someone would see those menus on the left side of the door and come looking for a deal.

41

It meant less work for her, so why was she so upset?

She set aside her water glass and went into the bar to dust bottles and inventory her stock. There was always so much to count in this place — women, barrels of illegal drugs, whiskey, money. What she wouldn't give to escape White Fog and never look back. She'd leave Alaska altogether if she could, simply so she wouldn't think of the people she'd known.

Two regulars came in to ask for the daily special, and she put in their orders to the kitchen and delivered their drinks. Then, with dust cloth in hand, she worked over each bottle of booze, forcing her thoughts into anything but what would take place today.

From the corner of her eye, she caught movement outside, and her heart tumbled three stories to hit the ground with a splat. A group of men were outside, reading over the menu.

Panic swept through her. For a minute, she contemplated locking up and turning off all the lights.

Out of the shadows came Max, his shoulders as wide as a ship's bow. He strode to the front and spoke to the men.

"Are you interested in something on the menu?" she heard him say to the newcomers, but she couldn't make out the response.

"We're closed." Max's raised voice reached her loud and clear.

"There are other people in there eating. I see them through the window," the man outside said.

Max turned his attention to her, and she gave him a nod. Whether they were here for pasta or to buy a Russian woman, Ruby's Place had it on offer.

Seeing her agreement to let them in, Max stepped aside. The first man seemed too wide to fit through the opening. He shouldered his way through. The guy behind him had to duck under. Ruby sucked in a sharp breath as one by one, eight men filled the room.

She nearly dropped the bottle she was holding but managed to set it atop the bar to wring her hands together. What they said to Max convinced the man that they were truly here for a meal.

He stood in front of the visitors, arms folded, waiting to see what they'd do next.

Realizing she couldn't just stand there anymore, she rushed around the bar to greet the guys. "Hello. Welcome to Ruby's Place. Will you be dining today?"

One man who appeared to lead the others eyed her. "Yes, we're here to eat."

"Of course. Take a seat anywhere. I'll just...grab your menus. I'll be right back."

Aware that they followed her every move, she grabbed some laminated menus to carry back. Chairs scraped across the wood floors and creaked when the big men seated themselves around the largest table.

43

Surely so many large men belonged to some club or organization. Maybe the mafia had sent them here to ensure she was doing her duty? As she passed out menus, she covertly studied them. None seemed to have the appearance of the other Russian men she'd seen before. Then again, how could she place a person's nationality by sight? She'd only heard one of them speak, and he didn't carry an accent, but that didn't mean anything.

She was too exhausted, and if she was honest, downright frightened, to analyze the situation. She'd feed them and send them on their way.

"What can I bring you to drink?" she asked, pulling a notepad from her apron pocket. She tried to control the shake in her hand that never seemed to fully go away.

Before the first man could answer, two of her girls walked downstairs and entered the space. They took note of the guys, whispered to each other and giggled. One girl made a show of pushing out her breasts, as if her skimpy top didn't already reveal enough.

These girls came to America with hopes and dreams. But they also knew they'd have to earn their bread and butter — at least until they were "married off."

That marriage came with an exchange of money, and whether or not the girls minded that, Ruby didn't know and tried not to care.

She threw the girls a pointed look to shut their mouths and took their drink orders, moving around the table to each man. When she glanced up, a big man had his stare centered on her as if she was the only woman he'd ever laid eyes on.

Her insides tremored. That trash can was sounding mighty good to her right now.

No, this wasn't her. She was tough.

She lifted her jaw and met his stare. "What can I bring for you?"

His very full, very sensual lips seemed to quirk in amusement as he said, "I'll have a beer."

"Draft?"

"Craft."

"Lager or ale?"

He was definitely smiling at her, the corner of his mouth tugging upward until creases popped out around his vivid dark blue eyes. "Ale."

"IPA?" She referred to an India pale ale.

"Actually, I've changed my mind. I'll have an iced tea."

She stared at him. After the banter, he totally changed his mind about having a beer. With a shrug, she moved to the next man at the table, who knew exactly what he wanted.

When she reached the kitchen, Anushka and Inessa had their heads popped out of the door, staring at the men. She shooed them inside and ordered

Anushka to fetch the gallon of fresh-brewed iced tea from the refrigerator.

"Are they here for us?" Inessa asked.

Ruby wanted to drill some sense into that pretty head of hers. Didn't they realize the hopes and dreams they had for themselves would end in a pile of ash and pain when they were purchased by some lowlife man, made to slave for him and bear his brats? They wouldn't be showered with diamonds and vacations and luxury cars. The Bratva lied to them to reassure them so they boarded the ship quietly.

Her insides curdled for five heartbeats before she gave Inessa a curt, "No."

After she had all the drinks loaded on a tray, she returned to the table. The guys took up so much space. Their muscular arms required so much elbow room. Their big frames swallowed the chairs.

She dispersed the drinks and then gathered her pad again to take their food orders.

"We're trying to find lodging in the area. It looks like there are rooms upstairs," the leader said.

"Oh. No. No rooms here."

The man didn't shift his attention from her face. Why did she feel as if she was being x-rayed right down to the marrow of her bones?

"Where can we find accommodations for a few nights?"

Panic swallowed her again. "Anchorage."

All eyes lit on her. Across the room, Max shifted his stance, spreading his legs wide in that don't-give-anything-away pose she knew so well.

The good-looking man with the dark blue eyes the color of a night sky offered a smile. "Nothing for us there, but this place seems interesting."

More freaked out by the moment, she thwarted their question. "I'll see what I can find out for you. Now what will you have from the menu?"

Unfortunately, her voice broke on the word *menu*, which only had Max stepping forward in warning.

Oh God, she was screwing up so badly. She needed to take their orders and retreat to the kitchen to collect her wits. As she worked, she noted the man with the beautiful eyes and hard, sensual mouth never looked away from her once. If they were here for women, it was possible he thought she was on offer. Wouldn't be the first time the mistake had been made.

After she got all their orders scribbled on the notepad, she hurried past Max.

He stopped her with a hand on her forearm. She tipped her head to meet his stare.

"Be careful," he said in a low tone.

She pulled free of his grasp and bustled to the front, where she removed the menus from the window.

"What the hell was that?" Gasper said under his breath. They all heard him, though.

"Something weird's going on in this place," Penn put in. "Just keep your eyes peeled for anything at all."

"I'm keepin' my attention on Big Ugly over there. What's his role here? Bouncer?" Broshears asked.

Without glancing around at the big man with the shaved head and biceps like a cement worker's, Gasper assessed him. "Maybe he's the owner. He stopped that waitress by grabbing her arm."

"That's pretty weird, you gotta admit." Lipton raised his water glass to his lips.

The Xtreme Ops team wasn't wearing military cammies or even the black performance clothes they wore on some missions. Today, they were acting as tourists come to the small coastal town of White Fog for a spot of fishing, but seeing the team dressed down wasn't something that happened often.

The girls who'd come downstairs sat at a table, folding napkins into an ever-growing pile.

"Am I crazy, or are those ladies folding far more napkins than will ever be used in this place?" Gasper's question received several answering nods.

As they sipped their drinks and waited for their food, a girl went upstairs and returned with two others.

"That makes seven women working this shift, if you include the one that took our order and the two peeking out of the kitchen." Penn set his drink aside.

"Seven women for how many customers? Seems suspicious," Broshears added. "And why didn't the waitress tell us to try the bed and breakfast up the street for a place to stay?"

Just then, the waitress appeared, bearing a big tray heavily laden with plates of food. She was thinner than most women, but she had a toughness to her, like she'd worked herself to the bone. Still, her luxurious red hair tumbled in waves down her spine to the dip of her waist, accentuating the curve of her ass.

She dressed all in black, and her pale skin didn't appear to have seen the light of day in a long time. Also, the shadows of sleeplessness lay in crescents under each blue-gray eye.

Gasper followed her with his gaze as she moved to the table and balanced the tray on her palm while handing out the meals of pot roast and pasta. When she moved toward him, she avoided his stare, but he didn't mind. That gave him a better opportunity to study her.

She was beautiful—and as nervous as a new recruit on a battlefield. As she set the plate before him, he noted five blue moons on her forearm.

Bruising from that thug who'd grabbed her arm before. Clearly, he made it a regular habit and bruised her in the process.

"What's your name?"

His question made her jerk her head around. She pierced him with eyes the color of a stormy sea.

"Ruby. I own this place."

"Great place you got here." He wasn't entirely lying—the place was nicely kept up and was welcoming enough. But the bad vibes pinging his radar warned of something darker beneath the homey atmosphere.

"Thanks." She didn't smile at him, only moved away quickly.

As soon as they were alone, he directed his stare to his captain. "Did you see the bruises on her arm? That asshole grabbed her before."

Penn gave a nod under pretense of tucking into his pasta with marinara and meatballs. "Do a little investigating. See if you can check the kitchen on your way to the restroom, Jack."

Gasper pushed his chair back. The girls folding napkins offered him smiles, which he returned as he veered around the room as if searching for the restroom. As he passed the kitchen, he paused to push the door inward. A hasty scan of the room showed him the two other women plus Ruby clustered near the stove, talking quietly.

"Toilet's that way." The rough voice brought Gasper around to face the bouncer.

He was big, but so was Gasper. They shared a glare before Gasper stepped around him and headed to the restroom.

He spent a few minutes pretending to use the facility before returning to the table. When he sat, Shadow threw him a grin. "You're slackin', Gasper. Getting caught by that dude for snoopin'."

"I'm beginning to question who's in charge here." He picked up his fork. The food wasn't half bad, and the team had a lot of digging to do in this town, but he got the feeling they'd walked in to grab a bite to eat and stumbled across something bigger.

Ruby checked on them once more, refilling glasses as needed and fetching an extra napkin. But try as he might, Gasper couldn't catch her eye again. She avoided him most, steering clear even when she walked by.

Penn made it clear to the team they shouldn't trust Big Ugly in the corner either. They didn't speak about their reason for coming to White Fog. Instead, they talked about the weather and the possibility of chartering a fishing vessel for a few days.

The girls finished their task of folding napkins, and they went back upstairs. A minute later, two different women walked down. When they entered, both threw the Xtreme Ops team sideways glances.

Suddenly, Gasper stiffened.

Penn's eyes slid to him.

51

"Did you just catch an accent from one of those ladies in the corner?" He feigned biting into a roll that had been left behind after they all pigged out.

Penn returned the question with his own. "Is my hearing going bad, or is there a lot of noise over at the bar?"

Gasper twisted to see Ruby at the bar, pulling down the same bottles she'd been polishing when they walked in. When she felt his stare on her, she sliced a look at him. Her brow cocked as if to say, "Do you have something you want to say?"

Oh, he did. He wanted to ask what was really going on in Ruby's Place. Why so many girls were scheduled to work during a nonexistent lunch rush, and why that asshole in the corner grabbed her arm hard enough to bruise her.

Why she was thin and not sleeping well.

What he wouldn't give to get her alone and make her talk, but judging by the shards of ice in her glare, that wouldn't be easy.

After lingering at the table for as long as possible to scrape as much intel as they could from the place, they found they didn't have much more to go on than before they stepped foot inside.

Penn paid the tab, and left Ruby a hefty tip. As they strolled out again, Gasper's mind returned to how she'd torn the menu out of the window. Like the sheets meant something.

He was always attuned to people he helped save...but this was somehow different.

She kept an eye on him like she was protecting him right back.

He shook off the notion as fatigue. He had nothing to be afraid of.

Next, they paid a visit to the bed and breakfast. The place was kept up nice, and the sign out front said vacancy. Penn went in to secure them rooms, but in seconds he came out again. After he did, an older man with stooped shoulders hustled to the sign and flipped it to NO VACANCY.

"Captain Penn Sullivan—pissing off old men in under sixty seconds." Gasper's comment was met with several chuckles from the guys.

Penn shook his head. "That may have been a record."

"What happened?" Lipton asked.

"He said he doesn't rent to men like us and we're better off going to Ruby's Place."

Gasper's brows shot up. "So we're definitely not wrong that more is happening there."

"And this guy doesn't like it either. He's probably our best bet for information, but he's clearly resistant to seeing us."

They walked from one end of White Fog to the other in minutes. Funny how there wasn't a hotel in a town that boasted tourism as their high point. There must be cabins or camping facilities they weren't seeing at the moment, but damn if Gasper could make out where.

"This is an odd place." Shadow walked on Gasper's three o'clock, keeping pace as always.

"It's creepy. Reminds me of a movie. I keep waiting for a big creature to loom up out of the sea and swallow us." He slanted a glance toward the sea, the choppy waves rolling with white tips from the wind.

"I want to go to Ruby's Place and visit the upstairs." Penn's comment brought them all to attention.

"You think somethin' else is going on? Like a brothel?"

He shrugged. "Dunno. I need eyes on the place."

"Easy," Gasper said in a light tone. "Since we can't find anywhere to sleep, we'll be on the sidewalk out front."

Shadow chuckled. "There's always the SUV, man."

Gasper eyed him. "If you plan on taking off your boots, count me out. I prefer the sidewalk."

The bruises on Ruby's arm flooded into his mind. "We need to check into that woman who runs the place."

"One step ahead of you, Jack," Penn told him. "I already texted Cora to start digging around."

"The woman didn't want us there. In fact, she wanted us as far from there as possible. She said we could find lodging in Anchorage."

Lipton, who always seemed to walk a pace in front of them, hung back. "Did any of you catch the names of any of those women employed there?"

They all shook their heads and remained silent. Gasper couldn't help but believe there was an undercurrent in that bar. Something unspoken, unseen.

"We should talk to some other locals," he suggested. "Maybe someone's willing to spill."

"Good thinking. Same groups as before. Split off and act like tourists."

Gasper wanted to head straight to the restaurant. He gave Shadow a nudge. "What do you say about grabbing that beer we didn't get before?"

"No drinking on the job."

"One beer. It gives us an excuse to sit at the bar."

Chapter Four

"So far, White Fog sucks." Gasper stretched his aching spine beneath the spray of lukewarm water of the truck-stop shower.

Between watching Ruby's Place, he and the guys had taken turns sleeping in three-hour shifts in cramped positions in the SUV and now their only shower was the terrible truck-stop facility that no amount of quarters dumped into the coin box would warm up.

A howl came from the shower next to his. "Shit. My money ran out and I still have soap in my eyes. Gasper, you got coins?"

"Fuck, hold on." He reached blindly for his towel and scrubbed his own eyes clear of water in order to locate the roll of quarters in his pants pocket. Buck-ass naked, he stepped out to pump quarters into Shadow's shower.

Seconds later, his buddy gave a sigh of relief. "Thanks, man. That shit burns. My eyes were already on fire from staying up most of the night watching men go in and out of Ruby's Place."

Gasper grunted. He hadn't seen it with his own eyes, but his teammates told him at least half a dozen men visited the bar, which should have been closed.

Figuring he was cleaner than he'd been many days in the line of duty, and that the kinks in his muscles weren't receiving any relief from the lukewarm shower, he toweled off and dressed.

Though they weren't yet dodging bullets on this mission, they weren't enjoying a relaxing vacation either. Sleeping in the SUV and taking a tepid truck-stop shower were on par for the job description. But sitting on a barstool for hours waiting for some tidbit of information that would help them stop the Russian mafia was altogether new territory, and the frustration for him was real.

Like waiting for days for a bomb to explode.

While he brushed his teeth, he considered everything he'd seen while sitting on that stool. First, the clock was ticking down—too fast. If they didn't step in before the girls were sold, they'd have a hell of a time tracking them, and the likelihood of getting them back was slim.

Next, the Russians wanted them gone, and the bouncers would easily run anybody off—except the Xtreme Ops. To make their lives easier, the team needed to get the bouncers out of there immediately.

Last, Ruby was nervous as hell. The woman didn't want them there, which only prompted them to stay right up until last call. He swore that Ruby had purposely given him warm beer, and she refused to meet his eyes, though he wanted to catch a glimpse of hers again to make out if they were really blue or gray. Irrelevant, but he'd been intrigued. By the end of the night, he decided that they were a combination of the two, a stormy flint color that drew him in.

That, along with her curves from behind, which he'd stared at most of the night. Judging by the woman's body language, she didn't want them in her bar. Which totally went against an owner's creed. No customers meant her business would close.

Unless she had another source of income, and the bar was only a front.

He'd also learned other things about Ruby...such as the sway of her hips that showed up in his dreams last night. And how she tucked a corner of her mouth in when she was thinking.

Most telling of all was her reaction to the bouncer who "worked" for her. She kept an eye on him at all times, pivoting her body to keep a better view of his position in the bar or restaurant.

Gasper's radar was pinging.

When Shadow walked over to join him at the sink, his eyes were bloodshot from the soap episode. Gasper chuckled through a rinse and spit. "It's not the Ritz-Carlton."

"Thanks for saving my eyesight. It felt like I had gasoline in my eyes."

"You'd do the same for me. I'm going in search of coffee."

"If their coffee's as warm as their showers, maybe you shouldn't bother."

Gasper stuffed his damp towel and toothbrush into his bag and slung it over his shoulder. "Let's hope you're not right. Hot coffee's the only thing keeping me on my feet right now. That and the prospect of a few painkillers. Sleeping on that seat was hell."

"Seems as if we'll have another night of it too, unless some miracle happens and we find what we're here for." Shadow stuffed the toothbrush in his mouth, cutting off more conversation.

Gasper strolled out of the shower room in search of steaming coffee and the rest of his team. He found a pot of coffee that looked as black as coal and had probably sat there all night. His team regrouped outside. A few of them held energy drinks, but nobody had a cup of coffee.

Broshears shot him a grin. "Knew you'd be the only person brave enough to test that coffee."

Gasper lifted the paper cup in a toast and took a sip. Everyone watched his face. Lowering the cup, he said, "Damn. It tastes like it was percolated through Winston's sock." He took off the lid and tossed the contents into a nearby shrub.

The guys laughed and fired jabs at the captain for not finding them better accommodations. Penn scoffed and brushed them off, though he didn't appear to be so fresh and bright-eyed this morning either.

"Anything to report from last night? Jack, did the bar hold any interest for you?"

Why did Ruby's curvy figure loom into his mind?

He shook his head. "I only learned that the woman's nervous and she dislikes that bald dude who works there. Shadow and I didn't even see the girls. They didn't come into plain sight."

"They might have been warned off it after we were in for lunch, or their trade keeps them tied up after dark." Penn caught Gasper's eye. He'd thought the same thing.

Broshears cast a glance at the building. "Where the hell is Shadow? He get washed down the shower drain?"

"He's battling blindness at the moment. Here he comes." Gasper lifted his chin toward the man.

As soon as Shadow reached the guys, they took turns ribbing him over his red eyes until he threatened to give them swirlies in the fetid truck-stop toilets.

"I'm starved, and there's only one place to grab a meal," Gasper said. "Unless any of you want to chance the breakfast burrito in there."

Penn compressed his lips. "We'll hit the restaurant and then figure out a plan on a full stomach."

The short walk to Ruby's Place earned them curious looks from anybody who actually lived in White Fog.

"Is it just me, or do y'all find it curious that it's good weather, yet there aren't actually any tourists in this town?" Lipton's question had them all searching the empty streets. Along the dock, a small fishing vessel bobbed on the waves, but only the captain could be seen on deck.

Gasper swung his stare to the biggest building in White Fog, two stories high and a simple rectangle in design. The sign for Ruby's Place was the most interesting thing about it, with flourished red lettering that was slightly chipped by the harsh Alaskan wind and sea air.

When they got close enough to see the front, he narrowed his eyes. "The menu's taped on the opposite side today."

Penn narrowed his eyes. "You're right."

"Think it means anything?" Gasper pressed.

"We're about to find out." Penn entered first.

Gasper swept a glance over the space. His stare landed on Ruby, standing near the kitchen door, fists knotted at her sides, either because of the sight of them or a reason yet to be seen.

When she met his gaze he felt a tug, like the end of a rope being pulled. He took a step forward, and her lips parted as if she needed to draw in more air.

He couldn't shake the feeling that if he got her alone, she might talk. Last night at the bar was too soon, and Shadow had been with him. But he had to try—as soon as possible. They didn't have any time

61

for fooling around when it came to the mafia. With every hour that passed, they dug their hooks deeper into US soil.

They all took seats at the table from the day before. He made sure to position himself on the end. Ruby would have to pass by him several times while taking orders and delivering food.

When she strode to the table, he took note of the stiff manner in which she carried herself. Her shoulders might be pulled back, but he'd bet a year's pay that every muscle in her spine was knotted. Her neck too.

She wore all black again, and he couldn't help but drink in the starkness of her clothes against her pale skin and red hair. The grave color also accentuated the hollows under each of her flinty gray-blue eyes.

He tracked her every stride as she crossed the room to the table. When she reached into her apron pocket to withdraw the notepad, he saw a small tremor in her hand.

Straightening in his seat, prepared to bash a bald head off the nearest wall, he kept his eyes on Ruby. Either she'd believe him too mannerless to stop staring or she'd see what he was trying to show her— that he was here. He saw her.

"Ruby."

Her head shot up when he spoke her name. Their gazes locked.

"What's today's special?"

Flinty eyes burned into him.

"Chili."

Her expression gave nothing away. So why did he have the feeling she was trying to tell him something?

She had to do something and fast. She couldn't survive the tension of another day where these guys hung around her restaurant and bar. She had hoped during the night they'd return to wherever they came from.

Dealing with her bouncers on a normal day was difficult enough, but they had been unbearable since these men walked into her bar and spent far too much time lingering over food and drinks. Then last night, those two had come in for beers, which they'd nursed so long it became evident they wanted something else. But since neither were asking to entertain one of the girls upstairs, and they didn't indicate they wanted the drugs from the barrels in the back room, Big Mike and Max were edgier than ever.

And they took it out on Ruby. They'd taken turns showing her the live cam of her beaten father.

She also felt stupidly worried about their safety. Even tough guys fell to the hands of the mafia.

Dammit, didn't these men have anywhere better to go than White Fog?

Luck was never on her side. Not since that fateful day when her grandmother's will was read and Ruby's Place became hers. Her name wasn't even Ruby — well, her middle name was. And Elliana Ruby Rynizski didn't have the same ring as Ruby Ryan in a business like hers.

She fetched drinks for the group of guys and placed them on the table. They all watched her too closely. So did Big Mike and Max. Both men stood with their backs to the walls as they analyzed her every move.

When Max crooked his finger at her to follow him to the kitchen, her feet felt weighted to the floor, but she dragged them one at a time across the room to follow the man.

She faced him, shoulders squared.

"Get rid of them," he ordered.

"How do you propose I do that? Tell them we're out of food? Start a fire in the kitchen?"

"I don't care how you do it — just move them away from here. I know they're the reason you didn't put the menu on the left side this morning."

It was true — she had expected the men to return, and she couldn't very well have men coming in to buy girls in plain view of the strangers, could she?

"We'll find another way to make the deals until they leave White Fog. Get word out that we'll put menus up in the back."

Max gave a shake of his head. "No good. The terms have always been this way, ever since the day your father tried to swindle the Bratva."

She inflated her chest but didn't release the hot sigh. It burned her lungs and hung in the center of her chest like a scorching sun.

Max leveled his stare on her. "Get. Rid. Of. Them."

"Fine! I'll think of something. Just don't do anything to my father."

"We'll see about that once you comply."

She whirled to face the girls working in the kitchen. Girls she cared about…tried to help by improving their skills the best they could. She taught them to cook if they didn't know how. She attempted to get a few words of English into them.

She even gave them better clothes by fiddling with the numbers in the books—at risk to her personal safety. If the Bratva ever found out… She didn't want to think what they'd do to her.

If she failed to comply, she wouldn't be able to protect the girls.

Anushka ladled chili into a bowl and set it beneath a heat lamp to stay warm while the rest of the dishes were prepared.

"You didn't put enough in the bowl." Ruby hurried forward and doled out more until the chili inched toward the brim.

Big Mike stuck his head into the kitchen. "Ruby, you have more customers."

She looked to Inessa. "Go take care of the new customers. Anushka's nearly finished with the food, and I'll take it out to them."

A plan formed in her mind. Her grandmother always told her that desperation made people think on their feet, and she found that was true today. She needed to shoo these men out of her restaurant—and hopefully run them out of White Fog. Maybe she could manage to achieve that goal today.

Inessa walked out to wait on the regular lunch customers, while Ruby paced between stove and door, peeking out at the big guys seated in her restaurant. They were testing her skills. It wasn't easy hiding all these women, convincing them not to be seen or come downstairs until after closing time. Making sure any gentlemen calling on them came in through the rear and were rushed up to their rooms.

Handling the bouncers developed with other skills—like keeping them happy while shutting down their advances for her to come to their beds. Once, they'd even asked her to join both of them at the same time. While some women might jump at the chance to wedge themselves between two muscled Russian men, she shuddered at the idea.

But how long would it be before they took what they wanted from her? They were already stripping her soul each day by showing her that livestream of her father having his fingernails ripped out.

With the strangers sitting in the bar last night, the man who'd come for the shipment had left emptyhanded too. She couldn't afford for the barrels to pile up in her back room. It was bad enough having such a big responsibility—half a million dollars' worth of heroin in each barrel added up if they weren't regularly moved.

She shot a peek at the office, where a photo of her late and beloved grandmother hung on the wall behind her desk. That particular Ruby never wanted this for her when she left her the business.

It would be easy to toss a dishtowel on the flames of the range burner, walk out of the kitchen, and wait for it all to go up in flames. Lately, that was the only clear way out she could see.

She still had a card to flip, though. Anushka placed the last plate on the tray, and Ruby hefted it. Bustling out, she forced Max to step aside.

Reaching the table, she caught the mundane chatter of men in these parts—fishing, fishing, fishing. Did men care about anything but their stomachs, dicks or casting a line?

Her insides trembled as she set the first plate down. The man thanked her. She offered him her customer service smile and moved around the table. When she reached the final man, the one who stared at her too much—and raised a lot of alarms in her too—her heart pattered double time.

Why did she feel the tension running off him? What did she care if her bouncers tossed him out? Not at all.

From the corner of her eye, she saw Max twitch his hand toward his side. Going for his phone to remind her what was at stake or his weapon? Either for her own sake or the diners' safety, she couldn't take a chance on it being either.

She grabbed the bowl and let the chili slosh over the side, dumping half of it in the man's lap.

He jolted to his feet as the hot liquid landed on his crotch. He jerked a hand, and Ruby stumbled back to avoid a blow.

But he centered her in his gaze, and in that heartbeat, she knew he understood more than she could ever hope for.

"Oh no! I'm so sorry." She grabbed for the napkins off the table and started dabbing at the front of his jeans.

He let out a groan and placed a hand over hers, stilling it. "I got it."

"The red sauce is going to stain your clothes. Please, let me pay for your laundry. In fact, I'll take you to the laundromat myself. Follow me!" Before he could protest, she rushed to the door and pushed outside.

She only had to wait a second before he joined her. A question lurked in his dark blue eyes, eyes that appeared like a whole galaxy swirled in them, but she only shot him a glance before turning and hurrying down the sidewalk to the laundromat.

Could her heart pound any harder? She glanced at her chest, certain she'd see the organ pulsating underneath her top. But her outward appearance gave nothing away. She hoped her erratic behavior would be passed off as good customer service to Big Mike and Max. She already had her reason planned out—her dear grandmother would have done the same thing if she'd made such a mistake.

The man walked a step behind her, and she got an itchy feeling that he watched every step she took. Thankfully, the laundromat wasn't far, and nobody was in there at this time of day.

Small blessings.

Once they entered, she went straight to a washing machine in the corner. "Put your jeans in here."

He stopped midway through the room. "Strip down right here?"

"Do you want me to pay for your pants to be cleaned or not?"

His stare on hers left her with a strange floating feeling she couldn't identify—and didn't want to, either. She pointed to the open washer.

Slowly, the man came forward. He stopped in front of her.

"Ruby."

The way he said her name made her feel he'd touched her insides, stroking them with a callused finger.

"Hurry," she whispered.

He dropped his hands to the front of his jeans. She didn't mean to drop her gaze when he unbuttoned them and unzipped the fly, but once her stare locked on the bulge in his boxers evident there, she forgot how to move her eyes.

She compressed her lips, breathing in the scent of laundry powder and clean clothes, warm from the dryer.

The man bent to remove his boots and step out of his jeans. His hard, muscled legs were endlessly long and sported dark springy hair all over. The US Navy tattoo on his chiseled thigh didn't go unnoticed by her.

He stepped out of the jeans and pulled a few items from the pockets, including a phone and weirdly, a roll of quarters, as if he'd come to her restaurant knowing he'd need to pay for the washing machine.

He dropped the soiled jeans into the washer. His stare never left her face. "What's really going on?"

She didn't speak.

"This is a strange town. That B&B owner mentioned some things—"

"There's some on your shirt. You'd better put it in too." She refused to look at him. Damn the man for using leverage like that to get her to talk.

But what if he could help her? Her father?

When he didn't immediately move, she reached for the hem. Again, he stopped her, trapping her fingers in his big, warm hand. She sucked in sharply and pulled free.

He continued to stare at her while he shed his shirt and dropped it into the machine too. "We're mixing lights and darks."

She gaped at him. "You care about that?"

"I care loads about doing laundry."

She blinked.

"Get it? Loads?"

Not knowing whether to laugh or cry, she threw him a desperate look. She didn't trust that the Bratva didn't have every corner of this town bugged.

She dug in her apron for some money, but the man said, "I got this." He thumbed a few quarters from the roll and slid them into the machine.

As soon as the noise of water covered their talk, she battled for focus, but the military tattoos branding his tanned skin wasn't helping matters. Her gut told her as much, so why was she surprised? Unless those men at her restaurant were bodybuilders or Olympians here for a spot of fishing, they had to be military.

"Ruby."

71

When she didn't meet his gaze, his rough fingertip slid carefully beneath her chin, and he used it to lift her head. Her insides shouted that this man needed to go before he wrecked the house of cards precariously surrounding her.

"What the hell's going on, Ruby?"

The heat in his tone—and the sweetness—sent a pang straight to her bruised, neglected soul. "You guys have to leave White Fog."

"Tell me why."

She didn't answer.

He took a step closer, bringing that hot, muscled, tanned and tattooed expanse of chest near her nose. "Ruby, who's hurting you?"

She gulped. "Nobody's hurting me. But you need to go. This town has nothing for you."

"Now that I'm getting to know you better, I'd say this town has exactly what we're looking for."

"Which is?" She chanced a peek at his face, but his stare sent a blast of heat straight to her core. With a shock, she realized she was putting her trust in this man because she was *attracted* to him.

Of all the dumb reasons. She'd let her libido take a chance on her fate?

"Okay, let me tell you what I see."

Her insides quivered.

"You run a business that employs too many women."

"Stop."

"Those bouncers are really running the place."

"Please," she begged.

Gently, he closed his hands around her twisting ones, holding her steady. He may as well be holding her up. She channeled all the strength she took from his touch to remain upright.

"Let me go." Her voice came out as a hoarse whisper.

He released her and she rushed away. She crossed the room to the lost and found box. As she rifled the contents, she was aware that the man followed her and stood inches away again.

"I don't even know your name." She paused with a man's shirt in her hand.

"Elias."

She shut her eyes and reopened them. "Elias what?"

"Gasper."

"Here." She shoved the shirt at him and continued to rummage for something to put on his mile-long legs. All she could come up with were some men's sweatpants, which were worn out and far too small for a man of his size.

"Put these on. I can't think with you so..." She waved a hand at his nakedness.

Was that an amused gleam in his eyes? He donned the shirt, the cotton overly stretched across his chest. His biceps threatened to burst the seams. A grease stain from the real owner was a darker gray that drew her eyes again and again to his rounded pec.

"Ruby, you're flustered. Stressed. Scared. What can I do to help you?"

She whirled on him so fast that he stopped with one leg in the sweats. "I told you! Leave. Don't come back!"

He pulled the pants on faster than she thought a man that big could move. She was right—the garment was too small, and the hems came to midcalf. "I'm definitely not leaving if you're in trouble."

"You don't know me. You don't have any reason to want to stay and help me."

"So you are in trouble. Who's pressuring you?"

"Just…" His blue eyes were boring into her mind, making all her thoughts leak through the hole he made. "I have to return to the restaurant. Look for the purple float."

He didn't even blink at what she'd said. "Purple float?"

She waved toward the sea. "Out there."

Before he came up with any more questions, she ran out. Seconds later, she found Elias on her heels.

Why oh why had she given him that clue? Why did she feel the need to *help* the guy when he'd only keep screwing everything up for her? He wasn't one

74

of her girls to take care of. His size and strength told her he could do that for himself.

Stupid. She didn't have to save the world. She didn't have to let down her guard with him either. No matter how sympathetic the looks he shot her.

As she flew past the men at the table, she noted the strange looks they were giving her—then giving their friend. One started to chuckle, and another went into a coughing fit as he choked on his drink.

"Ruby!" Elias called out before she could hide in the kitchen. "Can I have another bowl of chili?"

She kept walking directly to the kitchen. There, she grabbed the first thing she saw—a bag of cornbread.

She strode out and tossed the entire bag at him. "Enjoy your lunch!"

The guys erupted in laughter, and Elias's eyes warmed a bit, though they still held too much concern for either of their good.

Chapter Five

The salty air of the Bering Sea filled Gasper's lungs and gulls wheeled in the air, following the boat in hopes of a fishing net and some stolen dinner.

His thigh muscles engaging with the rocking motion sent him back to other missions spent on the water. He hadn't dived in a long time, and it was time to tap those skills.

"It's going to take us a week to find the purple buoy. How do you know the woman isn't sending us on a wild goose chase to get us away from town?" Lipton stood at the rail, binoculars pressed against his eyes, scouring the water.

"She isn't. I heard it in her tone."

"You don't know her. She could be a good liar."

Her expression as it had looked in that moment she told him about the purple buoy flashed into Gasper's mind. He grunted. "No. She's telling the truth."

"The only reason I'm trusting you right now is I've seen you talk the devil into telling us where hell's located." Lipton had his sea legs too, shifting with the rise and fall of the vessel.

Gasper grunted, keeping his focus on the waves.

"The captain's heading east. Says he's seen some shit out that way during his Coast Guard years," Penn spoke up.

The captain they'd chartered to bring them out here had fought smugglers in these waters for decades. When they asked him to find the purple buoy, no questions had been asked.

"So what did happen in that laundromat, Gasper? How did you convince Ruby to give us intel?" Shadow asked.

"I felt like a cad for pressuring her, but I brought up what the B&B owner said about her place. He basically told us it's a brothel."

"That would make anyone talk," Shadow said.

"I'm more interested to hear what happened to his clothes. He returned wearing those sweats that came up to his knees." Lipton never lowered the binoculars and continued to search the water.

Gasper didn't want to think about the surge of desire in his balls when Ruby had put her hands on him. The touch might have been fleeting, but only because he couldn't risk standing there battling a hard-on. He may not know Ruby, but he gathered that she wasn't that kind of woman.

"Broshears, Shadow, check the munitions." Penn's order had the guys moving toward the bag they'd brought on board. Not knowing what they were getting themselves into, or what they'd find at the purple buoy, they didn't come without enough gunpowder to do the job right.

"Jack."

Gasper shifted his attention to his captain.

"Ready your diving gear. The minute we locate anything remotely purple out here, you're going in."

"Yes, sir." While he scrambled into his wetsuit rated for diving in frigid waters, Penn flipped open a case and removed his own set of fins and a mask. The waters would be cold despite the milder weather in June, and they'd both come equipped with diving suits.

"We've got a purple buoy. Off the port bow!" came the ship captain's call.

Lipton whirled toward the port bow, and Penn stepped up beside him. "You have it in your sights?" Penn asked.

"Yup. There it is, just as the woman said — bright purple."

Penn snatched the binoculars from Lipton to see for himself. "Damn. Sticks out like an elephant in the ballet." He handed the binoculars to his second-in-command. "I'll inform the captain we'll be diving."

Gasper hurried into his gear, outfitting himself not only for the cold water but with combat gear. Who knew what the hell was down there hooked to that buoy, so they had to be prepared for any contingency.

Within minutes, they reached the float. Seeing the bright purple bouncing on the choppy waves had Gasper's insides tightening. Ruby hadn't led them astray, just as he guessed she wouldn't. He trusted his instincts in all things, especially humans. If he got bad vibes off someone, he erred on the side of caution while assessing what made him hesitate in the first place.

He didn't pick up any odd hunches from the beauty in the bar. Only thing he gathered off her were waves of fear. She was tied up tighter than a constrictor knot, and if he had to make a guess, she'd be equally difficult to unravel too. Difficult, but not impossible.

As soon as they finished here, he planned to go into her bar and demand she speak to him alone. It might take some threats to make the bouncers back off, but he had no doubt his team could handle the challenge.

A heavy weight settled in the pit of his stomach every time he thought about Ruby. At first, he told himself his attraction to her played no part in this game. But then the strong desire to cup her cheek and taste those full, plump lips had damn near overruled his good intentions in that laundromat.

Not to mention that he'd like to shove a handful of quarters into a washing machine and push her up against it to see her come apart for him.

Hell, now his perverted tendencies were popping out like hives. He liked watching his women get off. Toys, vibrators, and even various produce were common in his bed. What got Ruby's juices flowing?

His insides coiled with need, and he scarcely checked his dick. Couldn't fit a raging hard-on in a wetsuit, could he?

Penn appeared on his three, and he tossed his captain a look. "Ready?"

"Damn near." He would be if his thoughts hadn't taken the depraved path. Now that he'd thought about the washing machine, he couldn't stop thinking about it.

The captain had the engines revving to keep the boat from drifting too far away from the buoy. In seconds, Gasper was outfitted with a mask and air tank, his fins fitted to his feet.

He met Penn's gaze. The captain gave a nod. At the same time, they hitched their legs over the rail. Gasper balanced for a split second before dropping into the water. He entered as sleek as a seal. Quickly, he adjusted his air settings and pushed off through the water toward the buoy.

In their comms unit, Lipton guided them straight to it. Gasper concentrated on his breathing so as not to use too much oxygen from his tank. The goal was always to preserve because a diver never knew how long he'd be under.

The murky waters were illuminated slightly by their headlamps as they cut through the water toward the buoy. Crab trap floats were used often in the Bering Sea to mark where fishermen dropped their pots. Whoever had dropped the purple float must have something attached to it.

Penn gestured to Gasper. He kicked faster, propelling himself toward the object. His heartbeat picked up with adrenaline, and he slowed his breathing even further to control his heart.

With a final hard kick, he reached the buoy first. A rope dangled down through the water, shifting in the currents. Penn gave him the signal to follow it.

What was at the bottom of the rope? It could be a crab pot, and Ruby had tricked him. Or nothing more than a dangling rope.

They might find a bomb. It'd been known to happen.

He thought of Ruby's flinty blue-gray eyes and knew she wouldn't send him out here to be blown up.

He dived a meter and then another, ticking each length off in his mind. The hydro-static pressure increased the deeper he dived. His ears stopped up, his eardrums reacting to the pressure.

Then he spotted it. Penn did too, and they slowly sank deeper in order to reach it. At first, he didn't know what he was seeing. A bag of some sort, ballooning in the water like a giant jellyfish.

His initial impression was that this wasn't an underwater mine. The bag contained some other material, and he'd bet his bank account that it wasn't crabs.

Penn motioned, wordlessly cautioning him to be careful. Gasper gave a nod of understanding before he started working at a knot in the rope binding the waterproof bag shut. Long minutes later, he loosened the knot enough to peer inside the bag. It contained several more bags, all high quality and waterproof. He reached in and felt around with his gloved hand.

Bricks of heroin or cocaine. They wouldn't know until they reached the surface.

Propelling himself closer, Penn saw it and then pointed up. The bag was still heavy despite the buoyancy in water, but Gasper managed to knot the bag shut again, heft it over his shoulder and kick toward the surface.

Like a moth to a flame, he was drawn toward the ring of light above. Penn broke the surface first, with Gasper right behind. Hoots of celebration hit their comms. With Penn's help, they guided the bag to the boat. The captain tossed out a hook to reel it in. Gasper made certain the hook was solid in the rope before letting go — if it sank to the depths of the sea floor, they'd never retrieve it.

Then a life raft was lowered for him and Penn. They hoisted themselves inside, and it was lifted out of the water. Seconds later, when they hit the deck again, Gasper peeled off his mask first.

"Not surprised Jack's a fisherman now. I hope you brought us somethin' good." Lipton grinned at him.

Gasper leaned against the rail, stripping off his fins first and catching his breath. When both he and Penn were ready, two of the guys hefted the big bag onto a table where fish and crab would normally be sorted.

Penn gave the go-ahead, and Broshears sliced through the rope holding the bag shut. Shadow glanced in and issued a low whistle.

"Damn... Good haul." He stepped aside for Penn to see.

"Your informant did us a favor. The real question is why?" Penn pulled out a brick of heroin.

"That's the good stuff, too. Same as what they're finding in Anchorage."

"Yep, it's coming through here and being distributed. I'd say that's the reason for the high price of gas at the truck stop—the owner knows the people shuttling the goods are willing to pay the price," Penn said.

All the guys settled their stares on Gasper. "Again, why would she tell you this is here?"

Gasper pinched the bridge of his nose. "I can only think that the drugs are somehow hurting Ruby's business...or those girls who live upstairs in her building are connected to this. She wants it to be found out and stopped."

"Why did she trust you with the information, though?" Penn eyed him.

"Must be my devastating good looks." Truth was, he'd thought long and hard on it and came up empty too. She worked against him, but just when he thought she hated him, she did something like give him that clue to help him.

When she did that, she was leaning on him. Putting trust in his hands. Working together for both their good.

Penn snorted, and a couple of the guys chuckled. Then he searched for the ship captain. "Captain Bill, can you have the DEA meet us onshore? We'll hand off the drugs. Then we're heading right to the bar, and Jack can find a new talent when he picks apart the owner to find out everything she knows about where these drugs are coming from."

Gasper's heart kicked up again with another hit of adrenaline. Getting Ruby to talk wouldn't be easy. A hard woman came with a hard price, and this one wouldn't be wined and dined into telling him what he needed to know.

Ruby's spine hit the chair hard enough to force the air out of her lungs. Her fingers curled around the chair arms, and she shot a lethal glare up at Max.

"You can't push me around! I've told you twenty times—I don't work for you!"

His mouth twitched into a sneer as he pulled out his phone. She braced herself for what he was about to show her. *Please, let it be anything but my father's dead body.* She couldn't live with failure.

"You're going to listen to us, even if you don't work for us directly," he said in his rough English.

Behind her, the kitchen door opened. Whoever poked her head into the restaurant took a look at what was going on and retreated immediately. Ruby dug her fingers into the wood arms as Max thrust his phone in front of her face.

Her father lay crumpled on his side, face hidden, but his howls of pain echoed from the speakers and flooded each corner of Ruby's mind.

"Stop! I don't want to see." Her words ended on a weak rasp. She hated herself more by the second—she wasn't this woman. She stood up to anybody who screwed with her, but when it came to her father, her inner child surfaced, and she would do anything to make sure he was safe.

Though she'd asked herself plenty of times what he'd ever done to help her. Certainly when he was gambling away their money and damn near lost the bar too, her father didn't have her in mind.

A boot came onto the screen, swinging back sharply. Then the toe connected with her father's stomach. He groaned and fell still. Thank God he'd passed out, though what damage they'd do to him in that state, she didn't want to see.

"Get away from me," she spat at Max. She wanted to curl up and cry but held it in. Crying wouldn't get her father free before these bastards took his life, sold off all her girls…and God knew what they'd do to her.

"Those guys have been hanging around here a lot. Why?"

"I don't know."

"No funny business."

"They're customers. I run a business, in case you forgot."

Max met her glare with one of his own. She steeled herself for a blow, but he didn't hit her very often. Not since that night she woke him up dangling a red-hot cast iron skillet over his balls.

"You took that man to the laundromat."

"Because I dumped chili in his lap. My dear grandmother would have done the same to repay a customer."

At that moment, the front door opened. She held her breath, praying with all her heart that the man they were talking about didn't just enter her building.

Dammit.

Elias Gasper filed in first, shoulders filling the opening a split second before he pushed through. His dark blue stare swept over the room and landed on Ruby.

Was it her imagination or did she see Elias's jaw clench and the spark of fury in the depths of his eyes?

For a full heartbeat, neither she nor Elias looked away. Then she broke the connection and settled her stare on Max.

Max's eyes took on a gleam as if he knew something she didn't. "Make sure you don't dump any more chili."

Thinking fast, Ruby said, "Maybe I like how he looks," she said in a furious whisper.

Thankfully, God was on her side and Max lowered his voice too. "You want his cock?"

"Yes." She raised her chin.

With a chuckle, Max backed off and pocketed the phone. "Make sure you get rid of any brats, or we'll sell them."

Her stomach burned and twisted, but she didn't vomit at the dark promise. "I'm smart enough not to get knocked up by some drifter."

Max grunted and stepped away from her. Ruby realized he'd slammed her down into the chair, but she was free to stand now. She popped to her feet, and, ignoring the bruised sensation on her back, she hurried across the room.

Elias's eyes flew open wide as she latched on to his thick forearm.

"I have your clothes. From the laundry."

His eyes flickered over her face. Beneath her arm, she felt his muscles coil. Knowing full well that Max was watching her, she stepped closer to Elias. His masculine, spicy scent rushed in, and her mind reeled.

From the corner of her eye, she caught Max taking a step toward them.

Too late to back down, she realized what she must do or risk the bouncer catching her in a lie.

She very slowly, very purposely, rubbed her breasts against Elias's chest.

He froze like an ice sculpture, his stare locked on her. Her insides flip-flopped between nervousness and real desire she hadn't felt in...how long now?

Releasing him, she twitched her jaw. "Come with me."

As she passed the table of men, she called out, "Welcome. A waitress will be with you in a minute."

Without checking to see if Elias followed her, she strode out of the restaurant. The hallway linked the kitchen with her office and the laundry area. No sooner had she stepped over the threshold of the laundry room than Elias crowded behind her.

Surrounded by dirty sheets and towels, she had nowhere to escape his big, overbearing presence.

"What the hell's going on?"

She couldn't meet his eyes. "I'm sorry about out there. I had to make it look as if I have a thing for you."

His brows shot up, which emphasized his manly features. "Ruby, you better start talkin'. But first, I have to do this." Without warning, he hooked his big hand around her waist and tugged her up against his broad chest.

Her breath whooshed out, but she didn't have time to pull it in again before he kissed her. The pressure of his mouth and the flood of liquid heat sinking between her thighs was a hundred percent genuine. She didn't have to act for Max's sake when she issued a throaty moan and slipped her arms around Elias's neck.

With a grunt, he deepened the kiss, angling his head to crush his lips down harder, applying pressure to her spine with his fingertips. Oh God, she'd tempted the beast and now she was receiving what she'd asked for.

Did she want this? Elias was a stranger. Sure, she'd seen him half-naked and knew how hard he was from shoulder to strong calves. She knew his preferences for food and drink, but knowing these things didn't make him kissing material.

Except holy steamy hell, he was. Every sweep of his mouth across hers had her rising on tiptoes to wiggle closer. A shiver coursed down her spine, and he yanked her tighter against him, locking an arm behind her back to pin her in place as he switched the kiss to tender nibbles.

The soft caresses suddenly stopped.

A breathy sigh left her. She opened her eyes to find the man staring down at her with confusion and desire stamped on his rugged face.

"We found the purple buoy."

She dropped to her flat feet, but he didn't let her go, and she didn't tear free of his arms. It really had been ages since she let a man touch her. Maybe a whirlwind fling was exactly what she needed to break up the tedium and push away the constant fear in her life.

"Why did you give me that information?"

The question of the century. Right up there with if Mars could really be inhabited and what exactly was happening to the polar ice caps.

Her brow pinched as she fought to puzzle out a reason for what she'd done. "I-I can't think with you touching me like this."

A gleam hit his blue eyes. But they weren't only blue, were they? They were really like a night sky, a swirling galaxy.

"Well, I'm not letting you go, Ruby. Tell me why you rubbed yourself against me out there."

"That…" She wanted to sink through the floor boards. "That was for the bouncer's sake."

"Tell me his name."

Did she give his real name or his shorter, Americanized one? She didn't know Elias, so why should she place her trust in his hands? Just because her body felt good in those very hands didn't mean squat.

"His name is Max." It wasn't a lie—he answered to it.

"And the other one?"

"Big Mike."

"They don't work for you, do they?"

A hiccup of air lodged in her lungs. "I don't want to talk about them."

He studied her, his gaze roaming from her hairline to the point of her chin. Why was he looking at her this way—like she was a treasure hauled up from the depths of the sea? Her insides heated more.

Footsteps sounded in the hallway outside the laundry room. She didn't have time to peek over Elias's shoulder and see who it was, because he turned her so her back pressed against the dryer, his shoulders blocking her from view.

Barricading her. Protecting her?

She shuddered.

"Who are you really, Ruby?" He slid his rough hands up to her shoulders.

"Who are you? We don't know each other, and it needs to stay that way." Why did a stab hit her heart when she said that? She must be losing her mind, or he sucked it out with those kisses that weren't nearly deep enough.

"Talk to me, sweetheart. Give me something— anything. Tell me if you're safe here."

She shook her head. "I can't answer those questions." She reached behind her and laid a hand on his clothes she'd rescued from the laundromat. She shoved them at him. He spared the items a glance before taking them and dropping them on the floor.

"Why don't I tell you what I see? Will that make things easier on you?"

She gulped.

"I see a tough woman trying to hold together a business, but there's some undercurrent here. Something darker than bowls of chili and bags of cornbread."

She didn't speak. How could she?

"I see two bouncers in an empty bar. There's something funny with you switching the menu on the door."

She bit off a cry of despair. "Stop. Please just stop talking."

He eased a fingertip along her jaw and then cradled her nape. Her head tipped at the feel.

"And I see a beautiful woman who hasn't been touched…or kissed…" A puff of air rushed over her lips as he lowered his mouth to hers once again. "In a long time."

She surged onto tiptoe to crush her mouth to his. The wild need pulsing through her veins made her bold, and she grabbed at his shoulders, pulling him down.

He pressed the tip of his tongue against the seam of her mouth, and she opened to invite him inside. She wasn't prepared for his taste, though. Desire pounded through her. She locked her arms around his neck at the same time he picked her up and settled her atop the clothes dryer.

Elias flicked his tongue over hers, and they shared a primal moan even as he crowded between her legs, splaying them wider to accommodate his size. From the bulge of his cock against her pussy, she knew he was as big down there as he was everywhere else.

"Fuck, I can't get enough of you," he rumbled before his mouth slammed over hers again.

She cried out, rocking against him, needing more of this mindless pleasure. The images of her battered father on that screen and her fears for her girls upstairs faded in a meteor shower of heated kisses.

Raw power coiled in this man's every fiber, and she drew from those strengths. He could help her— he'd already found the purple buoy. And she knew he'd also found what was under it. The package that would have hit her back door by way of a barrel in a week or so. Then a few young women would be sold with the drugs, but now that couldn't happen, right? The drugs were gone, and the girls' leaving would be postponed for a little while.

Elias threaded his fingers into her hair, trapping her, tilting her head further in order to delve his tongue into her mouth in languid passes that left her quaking. Suddenly, he withdrew to stare at her hard. "You're so goddamn beautiful."

Her heart throbbed at his compliment, just as it had when he said he saw a strong woman. The fact he'd been in this shit town for mere days and saw her as more than a mule coerced by the men holding her father prisoner lifted her spirits more than anything had in far too long.

She wiggled closer. "Meet me out back tonight. In the garden."

"Nothing could stop me." He rocked his hips, bringing his hard length up against the V of her legs. Her pussy flooded with want, and she sucked in a gasp.

"Uh...Ruby?" The woman's voice shattered her sexual haze of sweeping kisses, whispered promises and callused hands.

Elias stiffened and tossed a look over his shoulder. "It's your waitress."

Reality struck hard as any blow. She wasn't being washed away in a current of pleasure with a hot guy — she was the granddaughter of the original Ruby, her father was a prisoner of the Russian mafia, and no sun would shine down upon her today or any day after this.

She met Elias's stare. His eyes still held the heat of their make out session, but he stepped aside to allow her to jump down from the dryer.

As her feet hit the floor, she snapped into her role once more. "Inessa. What do you need?"

"There is...something for you to handle. In your office."

The woman's eyes flicked from her to Elias. She knew better than to spill her guts in front of a stranger, so she waved for Ruby to come forward. She hurried to her side, and seeing her white face and pinched expression, she slid her arm around the girl's shoulders and led her out of the laundry room.

She took the girl into her office. The minute she saw what awaited her there, her stomach bottomed out. She rushed to the chair, where Jenicka slumped over.

Immediately, she grabbed the girl's wrists and checked for track marks on her arms. Seeing the injection sites, she jerked her face toward Inessa. "What happened here?"

She twisted her hands. "She claims a guy from last night wanted her to get high with him. Then she went limp on the stairs. I could barely move her into your office. What will you do, Ruby? We all know the rules around here—you get high, you're out."

Ruby straightened, staring down at Jenicka, who eyed her blearily. "She's out." She cupped the girl's face. "Do you hear me? You have to leave. You broke my rules—no drugs!"

"But where will she go? She doesn't have family or friends besides those in this building!" Inessa jumped to her defense, even though she told her about the girl shooting heroin in the first place.

It broke Ruby's heart to do it, but she had rules and couldn't have her girls using the drugs meant for the streets. Either way, this ended badly—with a girl alone in the world to forge her path through prostitution or worse, and Ruby would be left to feel like the murderer. Or she let her stay, and pretty soon she had a house filled with druggies. She'd learned the hard way that as soon as one girl tested her by using drugs, they all would.

She issued a shaky sigh. Elias's scent still clung to her skin, but she felt far removed from the woman who'd kissed him back with abandon.

"Pack her things and meet me at the back, Inessa."

"No! Ruby, please don't do this. She'll be alone to starve."

"I can't have people breaking my rules," she answered in a flat tone.

Jenicka, slumped in the chair, shot Ruby a grin. Clearly, she would be out of it for a long time. But when she came out of her drug haze, she'd find herself locked out of the only home she had here in America.

She stomped to the door and threw it open. When she called for Max, the man appeared instantly. He was never far away. He'd probably watched her kissing Elias and grinding on him, which was good for her cover.

She pointed to the young woman. "She must go."

Max nodded and moved to the chair. He tossed her over his shoulder and walked out.

Ruby watched her go, ignoring Inessa's noisy sobs. Any softness she'd felt a few minutes before at Elias's hands was long gone. She was Ruby again — hard and ruthless. A woman who had no choice but to do what would protect what she had and what she loved.

Was it worth it anymore?

Chapter Six

What the hell happened? He'd lost his grip—something he never, ever did. Years ago, he'd fought alongside plenty of men who did the same, and he didn't have any respect for their dalliances with generals' daughters or one-night stands with the wives of diplomats.

Ruby was neither of those things—at least, what digging he'd done on the woman matched what she presented to the world. Still, he wanted to kick his own ass for messing with her.

Kissing her had been as easy as breathing, though. Touching her body, lifting her, thrusting his tongue against hers, plunging his fingers into the thick mass of her red hair…all those moments had come so naturally that he didn't need to think.

But the expression of fear on her face when that woman walked in on them wouldn't quit revolving through his damn mind.

She'd told him nothing and everything in that moment. He and his team knew all didn't add up in Ruby's Place. Everything was off.

All appeared quiet. No customers came or went. The inhabitants didn't step outside for fresh air, take a walk or even peek out the windows. With a wall at his back, he raised his binoculars and scanned the front of the building.

He only sat there about an hour before the sky opened up and a storm swept in. Walls of rain pushed by the pressure systems of the Bering Sea struck him hard and soaked him to the skin. He could return to the truck stop and dry off, but his gut was tingling again, and it wasn't the food at Ruby's Place.

What people were on the streets would seek shelter in a storm such as this. So what better time for an illegal transaction to take place?

The longer he sat there, and the wetter he became, the more he knew with an instinct born of experience that he must stick it out. Sheets of rain continued to slam the streets, but over that din eventually came the noise of a truck engine.

He twisted his head to see up the street. Sure enough, the vehicle was rolling into town. In a town this small, a person quickly learned the regulars who frequented the laundromat or small corner store. He'd never seen a truck like this before. On the side, a logo stuck out to him.

A liquor delivery.

"I've got something," he told Penn through the comms unit. "I'm moving closer to have a better look."

"I just sent Winston to relieve you."

"Winston can come if he likes, but I'm not leaving this post."

He wasn't directly disobeying an order, but it came close. Why was he so invested in this mission? First he'd slipped up and kissed the hell out of a beautiful woman who may be enemy or informant, and now he was basically telling his captain to shove it.

He wasn't sorry, though. He ducked and rushed to the next building. Hitting his knees, he made himself small so as not to be seen easily through the slanting rain.

The truck downshifted. Gasper was close enough to see the flash of red on the pavement when the driver braked.

He had to move in, find a better angle. Running through the rain didn't bother him—he'd done it plenty as a kid, and he was from the land of ten thousand lakes. He swam so much that if he was dry, his family commented on it.

When he dropped to a crouch behind some garbage containers, the truck backed up to Ruby's. Someone wearing a black slicker emerged from the building, but he couldn't make out who it was.

Until the wind ruffled the hood the person wore, and he saw a bright red tendril of hair escape. Snatched by the wind, that red lock looked like a beacon.

He stared hard through the screen of rain at Ruby. She glanced around nervously as if expecting someone to pop out at her. Then someone got out and approached her. She quickly signed the clipboard he handed her before she vanished inside.

Seconds later, the tailgate of the truck lifted, and two men began to unload crates of whiskey and vodka.

"Whatcha got, Jack?" his captain asked in his comms unit.

"The bar's receiving a shipment of booze."

"Seems suspect. How busy is the bar? How drunk are the people of White Fog?"

"Have Lip run these plates for me. Alpha November Oscar three one seven."

"Copy that. Winston's approaching on your seven."

"Damn. Patch me in with him. I don't want to risk this driver seeing him."

"Will do."

Gasper clutched his binoculars. They weren't much good in this heavy rain, and the fog was rolling in to coat the ground in a thick layer. Evening was falling too. Soon it would be time to meet Ruby in the garden.

He wanted to kiss her again, but that couldn't happen.

He burned to pull her against him and make her trust him enough to tell him the real story.

Winston's voice filled his ear even as he signaled his coordinates from across the distance.

"I have eyes on you, Winston. What do you see?" Between the two of them, they might get a complete picture of the deal going down. Gasper didn't for a single second believe this was an ordinary liquor delivery.

"Two men unloading."

"That's what I got too. Any sign of the women who work here?"

"Negative."

Winston was often split from the main team of six and placed into a second team here in Alaska. The state was too big for one unit to cover most times, and Winston, Day, and Paxton, along with three others, formed the second unit. But since Paxton's injury, he may not be rejoining them, and that was a damn shame. Gasper would miss the hell out of the guy if he was sidelined.

More activity in the back of the bar caught his notice, and he peered through the rain and fog. After the cases were unloaded, a big wooden cask was rolled off the truck. He'd been in Alaskan bars enough times to know that wasn't normal. He'd never seen the likes of this.

"I can make out some letters on the side. Not all," Winston informed him.

"Good — we can use them to find out where the barrel's from."

"Got eyes on your girlfriend, Jack."

Gasper's chest tightened. While she wasn't his in any way, he couldn't help but wish he could get her the hell out of this place, far from whatever was going down on a daily basis.

At that moment, she moved across the short loading dock into the downpour. Her hood hid her hair as well as her face, but she walked up to a delivery man and shoved him in the shoulder.

"Oh fuck. Shit's about to get real." Gasper wanted to go to her.

"Should we put a stop to it?"

"Wait for my call." He stared at the pair. The man's mouth opened and closed in quick snaps, indicating to Gasper he was arguing. And Ruby slashed a hand through the air.

The man made a quick move, and Gasper half rose from his crouch, prepared to jump in if he raised his hand to Ruby. But the guy stepped away and yanked down the lift gate of the box truck. Without a backward glance at Ruby, he jumped to the ground, walked to the passenger side, and climbed in.

Ruby watched them go for a second before she vanished inside. The door closed, cutting off their view.

"How many women do you think work here, Jack?" Winston's question caught him off guard.

"Too many for a small-town bar with little business."

"Affirmative. I'm going to request that I remain in position, put eyes on the building. See who's coming and going."

"Good idea, Winston. Call for backup too, because I'm not waiting out here in the rain any longer."

"What are you gonna do?" Winston's voice held a trace of amusement.

"I'm going to knock and see if I'm granted entry." He straightened to his full height of six-two.

He raised his fist and knocked. Only a few heartbeats passed before the door flew open. Ruby stood there, still clad in the rain slicker, her thick red waves tumbling over the wet black cloth and her sweet lips twisted in anger.

"What are you doing here!" She glanced over her shoulder.

Gasper crowded into the opening, causing her to step backward. He glanced around the kitchen and saw they were alone, but a few boxes were on the prep table, a box cutter next to them.

"You invited me to the garden, remember?" He stepped toward her.

She backed away. "You're soaked to the skin. Did you walk here?"

"Only a leisurely stroll through the hurricane rain seeing what White Fog has to offer."

"And what did you see?"

104

Was it his imagination or had a worried light hit her eyes?

"White fog."

The corner of her lips twitched, but she dipped her head to hide her smile. "Well, take off your clothes. You know where the laundry room is. Stick them in the dryer."

He reached for his shirt buttons. Her gaze fixed on his fingers, and his insides clenched at the thought of what he could do to this woman simply by being himself. Plenty of women liked his appearance, but none smiled at his jokes.

Once he'd peeled away the wet outer shirt, he tugged off his black T-shirt. The instant Ruby's eyes landed on his bare torso, her teeth came down to sink into her plump lower lip.

"You don't even look chilled." Her voice came out a bit raspy.

He shrugged and bent to remove his boots before going for the waist of his pants. He never was a man for showing off to women, but he was aching and hard by the time he let his jeans puddle on the floor.

He stepped out of them. Ruby dipped her stare over his abs, stopping at his bulging erection tenting out his boxer briefs.

"I'm soaked to the skin." He reached for the elastic of his briefs.

Her gaze flew up to his face. "Don't strip down here! Go to the laundry room! You'll…find a clean blanket folded on top of the dryer. Wrap up in that while your clothes dry."

The corner of his lips quirked at how flustered she was becoming. And how cute she looked with that pink in her cheeks.

He bundled his wet garments into the crook of his arm. "Care to show me the way?"

"No, I do not care to. You shouldn't be here at all, Elias." The way she spoke the syllables of his name, all soft and whispery, left him no question that he'd thrown her off balance. Her kisses revealed how affected she was, and so were the tiny moans she issued each time he put his hands on her.

He lowered his stare over her body. Even in that wet slicker, she was gorgeous. Maybe a bit too thin — those curves would fill out to fill up his hands just right if he could alleviate some of the stress this woman was under.

Which was why he was here.

She bore the long, inviting stare he gave her, but not for long. She darted her attention to the box on the counter.

"Got a liquor shipment, I see."

"Yes." She forced strength into her tone.

They stared at each other for a long minute. He knew there was more, and she wasn't going to say. He knew when to back down from a standoff.

As he started past her to the laundry room, he paused and placed his mouth next to her ear. "What if I don't know how to work the dryer?"

"And here I thought you were a smart one. Guess you boys only get brains or looks." She clicked her tongue. "A shame."

Chuckling at her sassy retort, he strutted to the laundry room. But as soon as he entered, he found he was not alone. A young woman he hadn't seen before in the bar or restaurant stood there, leaning against the wall, watching the clothes spin in the washing machine.

She glanced up. Seeing him, she jerked from the wall and then struck a seductive pose with her breasts pushed up and her leg arranged like a model for a photoshoot, showing off the length of golden flesh.

He watched her for a second before opening the dryer. It was empty, and he tossed his clothes in, choosing to remain in his underwear even though they were wet too. He wasn't about to strip in front of this woman.

"Hello." He spoke out of the need to fill dead air space.

She only smiled and nodded at him.

He peered at her closer. It was impossible to make out her nationality — there were pretty brunettes like her all over the world. But the fact she wasn't speaking made him think she didn't speak English, or understand it either.

"Jenicka!"

The girl snapped to attention as if she'd been shot when Ruby's voice rang out.

The pair looked at each other. Ruby waved to the exit, and Jenicka ran through it.

No words had been exchanged, which only solidified his belief the young woman didn't speak English.

"Sorry about that. She tends to show up in places she isn't supposed to be."

"She's your employee?"

Ruby nodded. "She's still learning."

Since this didn't seem like a moment to share with the team, he removed his earpiece and set it aside. He edged up to her and pinched a lock of thick red hair between his finger and thumb, following the wave down to the end. "Why don't you tell me what's really going on here, sweetheart?"

"Why don't you kiss your own ass?" she whispered in a seductive tone.

He grinned. "Because I'd rather kiss your lips." He leaned in, letting his mouth hover over hers, giving her the choice. And when she closed the gap between them and crushed her plump lips against his, he felt the sweet surrender of the moment.

Growling low in his throat, he he dragged her into his arms. She'd removed the slicker in the kitchen, and the fitted white blouse underneath was low-cut enough to show off the creamy tops of her breasts and a hint of what he knew would be ample cleavage once he peeled the top away.

She slipped her arms around his neck, and he molded her curves to his body, plundering her mouth without remorse until she trembled.

He ripped his mouth away, staring down into her eyes. A storm lived in the gray-blue depths.

"Take me, Elias," she whispered with a knife edge of desperation. "Make me feel like a woman."

"Sweetheart, you're all woman," he drawled.

He shouldn't lay a hand on her, but damn if he could walk away from that invitation. The hum of the machines provided cover for the small squeaks she made as he captured her mouth and her nipple with his fingers at the same moment. Her small nipple bunched beneath his fingertips, and he swallowed her cry when he applied even more pressure to the needy tip.

He couldn't get enough of her sweet taste and sounds. When he pressed her up against the wall, kneading both breasts at once, he watched her glow of desire creep from her breasts, up her throat, then settle in her cheeks.

"You should be made to feel good every minute of every single damn day," he rasped, watching her face mirror the pleasure she was feeling.

"You make me forget who I am."

He bent his lips to her throat and sucked at her pulse point. She writhed, arching into his hands as he

109

pinched and teased her nipples through her bra and top.

"Who is the real Ruby?"

She sucked in sharply when he nibbled at her earlobe.

"I don't think I'll receive any answers from you, not in this aroused state," he grated against her ear.

She shuddered.

"And the only thing I want to know from you right this minute is whether or not you'll let me go down on you and eat your pussy."

She went dead still. He leaned away enough to see her pulse going crazy beneath her skin. Her flush intensified.

Then she grabbed his face and kissed the hell out of him. The little wildcat had him at her mercy, for damn sure.

His balls gripped tight to his body, and if they were blue, it wasn't from the chill.

He pulled his mouth free. Before he could issue a word, she planted her hands on his shoulders and shoved him to his knees.

He grinned up at her. "That's the answer I was hopin' for."

Ruby was melting into a puddle, even though Elias was at her feet and not the other way around. Each swipe of his hot, rough tongue through her slick folds had her gripping the appliance behind her for purchase.

Still, she nearly buckled when he spread her thighs wider and ducked to thrust his tongue into her pussy. She cried out, flooding him with juices of want. When was the last time a man made her feel this way? Unraveled, undone...un-everything.

Her mind was blank to all her cares waiting for her outside of this room and she didn't give a hot damn about anybody right now besides the man sucking her clit like he'd made it his life's work.

He wrapped those magic lips around her nubbin and with soft pulls drew her to her tiptoes. She tossed her head with a cry of ecstasy. The stubble on his jaw drove her crazy and at the same time raked against her sensitive inner thighs. His tongue, long and perfectly skilled in the art of giving great cunnilingus, might be Elias's best feature.

Right after his deep eyes, hard lips and harder body.

When she looked down at him, she found him looking back, his eyes pinning her. As if she ever wanted to slip away. Her grandmother's legacy could go up in flames, but she'd never walk away from how Elias was making her feel.

Like a woman. Part of the universe of flesh and blood humans who actually allowed themselves things like emotions and pleasure.

He snaked his tongue through her folds to sink into her cavern once again. She widened her stance and grabbed the back of his head, forcing him deeper. His approving growl was enough to make her lose it.

Shocks of electricity hit her core. She bottled a scream, not wanting a bouncer to come running, rocked her hips forward, and came on Elias's tongue.

"Mmmm." He bathed her clit with her juices, spread by his tongue, and sucked the bundle of nerves as waves beat at her system. She twisted her fingers in his short hair and rode her orgasm to the last shudder.

But he didn't immediately draw away as most men would. He continued to watch her face and lap at her pussy. When he reached up and latched on to her nipples, white-hot need hit her for a second time.

She didn't expect this orgasm. It hit out the blue. It rocked her world and pulled his name from her lips. Maybe it was the roughness of his fingers and the hard tug on her nipples or the fact he wasn't walking away from giving her pleasure until he was damn well finished that sent her sailing over the edge.

Gasping, trembling, she hung forward, hands still clasped around his head. Slowly, he brought his long, slow, thorough, insanely hot licks to an end and drew his tongue from her drenched folds.

"Feelin' good, sweetheart?"

She couldn't find any breath to respond with.

With a touch much gentler than a man should be capable of with those big hands, he eased his fingertip over her slit, up to the bump of her clit. As he pressed down on it, she jerked upright, her toes curled again.

"Oh my God! You're driving me crazy!"

"Good," he murmured, shifting her ultra-sensitive flesh under his fingertip right and left, dragging more moans from her. She wanted him to pick her up and carry her to bed and keep her there all night long.

She wanted to explore his body with her fingers and tongue in the same manner he was learning hers. And she wanted to watch his face as he came apart for her.

"That first day in the laundromat…"

She met his heated stare. "Y-yes?"

"I wanted to do this. I wanted to watch you come for me. To let go. But my first thought was to hold you against the corner of the washing machine and see you get off that way."

Shock hit her system at his dirty words.

"After you were soaking wet, I wanted to lick you right here." He licked her from hole to clit.

She cried out.

"Lick you clean. Make you come on my tongue. My fingers. Then start over."

She couldn't think or breathe. What was he doing to her? A complete stranger, yanking things from her she never knew existed. She was like that sea out there off the coast of White Fog, the depths unknown even after years of exploration.

"Elias!"

He latched on to her nipples again, pinching hard enough to make her cry out. How did he own every part of her without knowing her? Hell, he didn't even know her real name—and never would. He'd be gone soon, and she'd return to the dull monotony of daily fear and bullying by the Russian mafia.

But for now…she had this big, beautiful god of a man wearing an expression of determination on his handsome face.

He pulled a third orgasm from her. As the dizziness of bliss blanked her mind, she realized he'd lifted her. He caught her lips. She tasted herself there and kissed him back, holding on to his broad shoulders.

She yanked free of the kiss. He'd set her on the top of the washer and dropped his briefs. The veined length of his cock made her shudder with desire.

First, Elias cupped her cheek in his hand. "Will you have me, Ruby?"

The intimacy of meeting his eyes and saying yes almost broke her. She mentally floundered for a moment while he waited for her answer.

"Condoms are in the cupboard over the dryer."

If he was surprised she stored them in the laundry room—or that there were a dozen boxes there—he didn't reveal it. He pulled a packet out and deftly tore open the wrapper. With a hard jerk of his fist over his impressive girth, her eyes threatened to roll upward.

She'd never had a man like Elias and never wanted one as much. And for the first time in ages, she felt alive. Like more than just a survivor.

She hooked her ankles around his body and pulled him close. Cradling her face, he met her stare as he fit his cock head at the quick of her. In a slow, easy glide, he filled her, stretched her and stole the last remnant of her mind.

With each pass of his cock through her tight, hot walls, another rumble filled his chest. No sooner did he release the animalistic noise than another took its place.

She rocked into him, and he ground his hips in the rhythm of the machines around them. Right now, the only drive in him was to keep her safe and make her happy. Surely that was odd, right? He'd barely hit White Fog before some immediate need to protect Ruby had taken hold.

He twisted his tongue against hers, collecting each and every moan she made to store away in his memory. This may never happen again. A woman like her might only give herself once and then walk away without a backward glance.

Hell, he hoped that wasn't the case. Now that her flavor lived in his memory, he wanted more of it—and more of this clenching heat from the base of his cock to the tip.

Gathering her to his chest, he cuddled her close, absorbing her tremors of pleasure that rocked him to the bone.

"You're a...damn pervert...Elias."

A laugh bubbled from him. "Why is that?"

He didn't know he loved a woman who talked during sex until this moment either.

"Thinking of me getting off...oh God, that feels good...on the washing machine."

He angled his hips to hit her G-spot. "We can try it next, sweetheart. Right now, cum is boiling in my balls and I'm about to blow."

She dug her blunt nails into his shoulders and rocked faster, taking the lead while the explosion coiled at the base of his spine. When it rocketed up from his balls to jet out in long, thick spurts, he locked eyes with Ruby and let go.

While he caught his breath and stabilized his mind, she shoved her hands into his chest, moving him an inch. But he refused to budge from his position with his arms around her and his cock still buried inside her.

"You shouldn't have come tonight, Elias." Her sweet voice was quiet.

"You invited me, if you'll remember."

116

"It was pouring rain. What man comes to a date in the garden when it's pouring?"

"I do. You'll find I don't walk away from any challenge." He caught her eyes. The inner depths shimmered with something he wanted to examine closer.

She managed to shove him away from her and hopped off the washing machine. "You guys need to leave White Fog."

Still humming from his fucking amazing release, he eyed her. "Is that a warning?"

"Yes," she said without prevarication, reaching for her top. She yanked it over her bare breasts, but not before he noticed the pink, hard tips begging for his lips.

Chapter Seven

Frost had glazed the sidewalk out front of Ruby's Place, and a traveler had tripped on it and fallen. While Inessa took the poor woman inside, cleaned the scrape and bandaged it, with lunch on the house, Ruby carried a bucket of soapy water outside to splash on the concrete.

It took two buckets before the small bloodstain washed away, and she stood back, watching the water trickle off the curb onto the road that led through town.

Her focus today was off. She was never off. She couldn't afford to be. Too much rode on her shoulders.

When the sound of male voices reached her, it was too late to turn and run inside, slam and lock the door. Her distraction meant she'd allowed the guys to sneak up on her.

And Elias's stare fixed on her from twenty paces away, his eyes glittering and face serious.

Panic took hold, and her feet grew roots, sinking deep into the sidewalk. She held the bucket. Maybe she could throw it at them and drive them away.

But she stood there watching them come toward her, and she couldn't stop looking at Elias either.

Had he always been so big? Of course he had. She felt how big he really was deep in her stretched, slightly sore walls today. It had been bugging her ever since she woke and felt the effects of his loving yesterday in the laundry room. He'd given her four orgasms. Four. Who did that?

He'd been so far gone during his release that she didn't know if he even realized she was contracting around his length, milking the cum from him.

As the men filed past her and into the restaurant, she inwardly groaned. She didn't know their names, but all that mattered was they were meddling with her business. When Elias entered the kitchen and saw those boxes on her counter, she'd damn near died of a heart attack.

She managed to use her attraction to him as a way to deter him from snooping. But the fact was, her attraction had almost gotten her in deep trouble. After she was alone, Max and Big Mike cornered her to pressure her about the encounter both men knew had taken place.

The bastards. She couldn't even steal a private moment of pleasure with a hot guy without them discussing it. They also made sure to show her video footage of her father trying to eat and being sick. Both left her own stomach twisting.

She sucked in a deep breath as Elias passed her. He didn't pause to whisper in her ear or talk dirty about washing machines, which she'd never look at the same way again.

Clamping her hands into fists, she realized she still held the bucket. She followed the men inside and hurried to the kitchen. When she stood over the sink, panting hard, Anushka placed a hand on her shoulder.

"Are you okay?"

"Yes. I need a minute."

Anushka nodded and moved off to her post at the grill again. The lunch rush was nowhere near large, but she still needed to get out there and help take orders, bus tables and generally try to ignore the man she'd fucked.

Spinning from the sink, she waved at Anushka. "I need a slice of pie to give to our injured lady."

"Sure, what kind?"

"Go with the apple. It's freshest."

As Anushka sliced the pie and dished it out on a plate, Ruby tried to steel her resolve to go out into the restaurant and face Elias.

She took the pie. With a toss of her head, she stepped out. The minute her boot crossed the threshold, Elias pinned her with his stare.

From the corner of her eye, she saw his buddy nudge him. Elias didn't move, but he said something that had the guys laughing. She'd only experienced a small bit of his sense of humor, yet it did break up the tedium, didn't it?

Quickly, she hurried to deliver the pie to the customer with the scraped knee. She spoke with the woman for a long time, learning she was visiting Alaska on a twenty-day tour that might turn into a month if she got her way. At this, her hubby, seated next to her, smiled in a fashion that made Ruby see the pair of older folks were still very much in love.

Was that real? Her own parents…hell, she could hardly recall them being together. Her mother died young on an icy Alaskan road, and though Ruby knew her father had girlfriends and mistresses, he hid it well from her.

She'd spent most of her time in the kitchen with her grandmother, learning how to cook and run this establishment.

She knew nothing of marriage or romance or… Gahh, why was her brain even going there? She wasn't marrying anybody, least of all a stranger she'd let into her panties after a few steamy kisses and hot promises.

He raised a hand and beckoned her to their table. Panic hit her chest, and she struggled to take a breath, because all she could smell was his masculine, clean musk. She'd showered twice since he left just to try to rid herself of that scent, and though it was unlikely she smelled him now from clear across the room, her mind was trying to play tricks on her.

The other girl who was taking a shift waiting tables was tied up with other customers. For a minute, Ruby contemplated ignoring the guys and returning to the kitchen. But her grandmother's voice in the back of her mind pushed her feet across the floor.

She stopped at the opposite corner to where Elias sat. He never moved his stare from her, and her nipples betrayed her by peaking into tight nubs meant for the pinch of his hard fingers.

"What will you have?" She brought up her pad and pen.

One by one down the line, the men gave their drink preferences. When she reached Elias, he spoke up, "I'll have something sweet. And shaken."

Oh God. Why was he torturing her?

Heat burned in her cheeks. She refused to meet his gaze as she wrote down *tap water* and bustled from the table.

Minutes later, still shaken herself, as he knew she would be, she returned with the drinks. She set each glass before the men. A couple teased her about the special being spaghetti and meatballs when it was Friday, and shouldn't they have fresh fish off the coast?

She joked with them and finally reached Elias. She set the glass of lukewarm water in front of him.

He took a look at it and the corner of his lips twitched.

"That's not what I ordered."

"Can I bring you something else — like your bill?"

He reached for the glass. Why did she zoom in on his callused fingers wrapped around the glass as he brought it to his lips, or how his throat worked on a swallow of the liquid?

He set the glass down with a smile for her. Some of the guys snickered.

"I think we'll be staying a while. Maybe do some karaoke?"

She arched a brow. "We don't have karaoke."

"We're pretty good at making our own entertainment." He cocked a brow back at her.

Inside, she groaned. And twisted up in knots. And burned for him.

"The waitress will be with you in a moment." She spun from the table and made a show of going to the register and finding they needed more change.

"I'm going down to the laundromat to get some quarters," she called to her girl.

As soon as she walked out, she knew Elias would follow, and she wasn't mistaken. He caught up to her in a few long strides and he hit the doors of the laundromat right after she did.

When he caught her arm and whirled her to face him, she felt her resolve to distance herself flow away. He searched her face.

"Elias, you don't know what you're doing. You guys have to leave White Fog."

He pulled her closer. His big chest heated her through her top. "Tell me why, Ruby."

"This is bigger than me."

"I won't go until I understand how to help you and what I'm up against."

Her chest heaved. Her skin prickled. Her raging hormones got the better of her, and she couldn't stop herself from throwing herself at him. He caught her in his arms and slammed his mouth over hers at the same second she rose on her toes to meet him.

The sound of the laundromat door opening and closing tore at her senses. Then someone cleared their throat.

Elias let her go and glanced over his shoulder. When she spotted the state trooper standing there, her bowels turned to water.

"Can I help you, Trooper?" Elias wasn't a bit cowed.

"I'm here for Ruby."

Her eyes bulged. "For me? What did I do?" Her heart raced faster and faster, leaving her weak and nauseated.

Someone must have seen the shipment arrive last night. Or one of the girls spilled her guts to a paying customer.

Oh God, her father would be beaten for her slip-up.

The trooper stepped toward her and pulled his handcuffs off his belt. "We received a complaint from a young woman who says you threw her out on the streets without food or money, knowing full well she couldn't gain assistance."

Her mind reeled. Jenicka had turned her in? Anger struck. *How dare she?*

"She knew my rules about taking drugs under my roof. I sent her away."

"She says she was under your care."

"Well, she's not anymore." Ruby raised her jaw. Beside her, Elias was frozen stone.

"The young woman is underage, which means you'll be charged with endangering a minor."

"Under—" The word cut off in a slurry of cuss words her grandmother would wash her mouth out with soap for. She didn't know Jenicka was underage. The girls were all supposed to be adults, but of course, what did the Bratva care?

"I'm afraid I need to take you to the station with me."

"Son of a bitch," she murmured under her breath. "Fine. But at least let me call my restaurant and let someone there know I won't be back this afternoon."

125

When the trooper eyed her, she lifted her jaw in defiance. "It's lunch hour."

"Fine."

Within minutes she was bundled into the back of a car. Elias's face passed in front of her as he leaned in the opening.

"Ruby, I'll meet you there. Okay? I'm sorry for this. There was no other way."

She blinked at him, stunned with shock as she was shut inside the back of the car. She sat there handcuffed to the seat so she couldn't escape.

The only man she thought she might be able to put her trust in had betrayed her by having her arrested.

"She's never gonna trust me again. I fucking betrayed her." Gasper dug his fingers through his hair. The urge to fight, to inflict pain on someone, was overpowering, and he dropped his fists onto the table with a bang that made his captain look up.

"You didn't have a choice. We needed to get her alone."

"By having her arrested?"

"You know we had nothing to do with that. The girl called the cops."

"Fuck!" Gasper shoved from the table where he and Penn sat waiting for the trooper to book Ruby so they could talk to her. Offer her a deal.

This morning, the perfect storm had hit, and the Xtreme Ops team never let something this good go. They needed Ruby on their side to squeeze more information from her, but the only way to do that was to get her away from her business. Then they received intel about the warrant out for her arrest for child endangerment, and well... Penn's plan might be solid, but goddammit, Gasper didn't like it.

He paced between table and window. This small state police barracks wasn't even in White Fog but the neighboring village an hour's drive away. But all over the world, these rooms were the same. Meant to drive a person crazy if they sat here too long, and he had. He needed out of this place, out of White Fog.

That meant leaving behind Ruby.

If he hadn't just seen the betrayal and hurt on her face, he might believe he could persuade her to leave with him. He'd fucked that up good, hadn't he?

"You're getting too damn close to this mission, Jack."

He sliced a glare at Penn. "You're one to talk. I remember hearing moans coming from your tent in the middle of that storm when you first met Cora."

Penn didn't rise to the taunt—he knew Gasper well enough to see he was itching for a fight. He only watched Gasper pace to the window and back. To the window and back.

"Is that what this is?" Penn finally asked.

He stopped in his tracks. "I don't fucking know."

"Have you fucked her?"

Leave it to Penn. He never beat around bush and got straight to the crux of the matter.

"Yeah, I did. But there's more than sex." Now that the words were out, he couldn't suck them back in. Hearing them with his own ears forced him to analyze his emotions.

"You sure she isn't playing you?"

"She's not." His voice came out gritty.

"You don't know what she's capable of. If she's working with the Bratva, like we believe—"

Gasper lifted a hand and massaged his temples. His head ached, and it all started when Ruby walked out of her business under her own steam and stepped right into the trap laid for her.

"If she's working with them, she has a reason."

"And you know this reason?"

"No."

"Take a guess. You're the jack-of-all-trades. Surely you can read between some lines."

He dropped his hand to stare at his captain. "I'm not a mind reader and I can't predict the future."

"My guess is she owes them money, and they're using her restaurant as a trade center."

128

Puzzle pieces were scattered at their feet, and they could stick a few together, but the big picture wasn't yet visible to any of them. Least of all to Gasper, who was looking with his heart.

Dammit, yes, he was into Ruby. Acknowledging that much eased something inside him, a flutter of panic edged with adrenaline. He walked back to the chair and dropped into it.

No sooner had he sat than the state trooper stuck his head in. "She's all yours."

He swallowed hard and then shoved to his feet again. Before they followed the trooper to the room where Ruby was being held, he exchanged a look with Penn. Gasper didn't even know what he wanted to convey to his captain—he just didn't want him saying anything about their discussion.

Penn gave him a nod. Feeling more assured that his captain didn't plan to tell Ruby anything about what had been confided, he strode out of the room.

Seconds later, the trooper showed them to another room. Gasper entered first. As soon as he set eyes on Ruby sitting there with her head bowed, his heart gave a hard jerk, and he took a fist in the gut. Christ, there had to be some other way.

But if so, he couldn't see it. He'd just have to make the best of the path they were on.

She didn't glance up at him or Penn when they sat across from her. Under the fluorescent lights, her hair took on a strange cast that muddied the red hue. She was pale and her expression carefully set in stone.

"Ruby, we're here to help you," Penn spoke up first.

The glare she sent them might as well have been a bullet for all the force behind it.

"Anything you say in this room stays between us." Gasper pitched his voice low.

"You had me arrested."

"That girl you cast out of your restaurant made the call. We just—"

"Saw an opportunity and took it? What are you guys really here for?"

Gasper shifted. "What's really going on in Ruby's Place?"

When she didn't speak, her lips twisting as if to contain anything that might fly out of her mouth and convict her, Penn shifted in his chair.

"Look, Ruby. We know the Russian mafia is operating in these parts. You have a lot of women 'working' for you. We've seen a shipment delivered to the bar."

Her gaze jerked to Penn.

"And you sent us to that purple buoy knowing full well what we'd find there. I know you're scared— the Bratva is one of the deadliest organized crime groups on the planet. But it comes down to you letting us protect you."

130

"Who are you?" Her voice rose on the question.

Gasper set his palms on the table, fingers slightly spread in a gesture of truth and honesty. He needed Ruby to trust him again, because she didn't have many other options. Her time with the Bratva was coming to a close, and he'd seen what the group did to people who crossed them.

"We're a special ops team based here in Alaska, sent to handle terroristic acts on home soil."

She settled her stare on the center of his chest.

"We've been driving the Bratva out of Alaska for a couple years now. But they have a strong foothold. We know they smuggle drugs and weapons and women. And we're pretty damn sure at least two of those move through your business."

She paled even more, which only made her hair appear brighter. Christ, he wanted to help this woman on a level he didn't understand. Helping people, protecting them, was his job. But Ruby took that drive to a whole new level.

"What do you want from me?" The vitriol in her voice cut through the silence.

Gasper couldn't fucking say it. He sat back in his seat, indicating that Penn had the floor.

His captain leaned his elbows on the table and laid it out for her. "You can either become a criminal informant and aid us…or you can be charged as a co-conspirator."

She slammed her mask back in place, cutting off any view of her emotions on the matter. She might as well be the rocky shore out there along the coast of White Fog for all her expression gave away.

"That's no choice at all."

"Ruby. We want to help you," Gasper said.

As her stare met his, his chest swelled with that almighty need to keep her safe above all else.

"You can do your best, but we both have dealt with the Bratva long enough to know that we're on the losing end of this battle. What choice do I have? You've bound my hands."

"We can unbind them. We just need information, and this all goes away."

She glared at the ceiling. Gasper wouldn't be surprised to see twin scorch holes in the tiles.

"Fine. I'll help you. But like I said, we're all screwed."

He should feel good about her agreeing to give them information, so why did he feel they'd all just boarded a sinking ship?

They had fragile ties to untangle here. Somehow, they had to eliminate the hold the Bratva had on Ruby without getting her killed.

"What are they holding over your head?" Penn asked.

She barked a harsh laugh that tore at Gasper's heartstrings. She pinned Penn in a look and then shifted it to Gasper.

"They have my father."

Fuck. That was pretty strong leverage, and it rarely ended well. Actually, Gasper had never seen a case like this end well. Typically, the minute the mafia became aware that the Xtreme Ops was coming for their prisoner, they offed him.

"Tell us how that came about," Penn said quietly.

"My father was stupid. He gambled and owed them. Isn't that always what happens to idiots who get snatched by the mafia and held against their will? He isn't a bright man — in fact, he's weak. But I still have to keep him from dying, don't I?"

Gasper noted the hitching breath she took and knew her tears weren't far from the surface. "You're doing what you know how to do, Ruby. Now tell us everything, starting with your real name, because we know you're operating under an alias."

She closed her eyes. "My middle name is Ruby, after my grandmother."

That was in line with the intel they had.

"My given name is Elliana Ruby Rynizski. I don't want to claim my father's last name, considering what he did, and Ryan seemed close enough."

Gasper caught her eyes and gave her an encouraging nod. Coaxing people to spill their stories was the worst part of the deal. Emotions and trauma ran high in these people. What he wouldn't give to heal Ruby right now.

"Where is your father being held? Do you know?" Penn asked her.

"Russia. They beat him. Starve him. He's ill, wasting away."

"And they tell you this?"

"I see it with my own eyes."

"How?"

"The bouncers show me a live feed on their phones."

Hell, this was growing worse by the minute.

"If you know how to pay my father's debts, they'll free me from the agreement and return him to the United States."

Gasper doubted it, and judging from Penn's silence, he did too.

"Ruby, we're going to do everything we can for your father. What you've told us helps. Now we know what's at stake."

"My father's life!"

Gasper wanted to stand up and circle the table, take her in his arms and tell her it was all going to be okay, but he couldn't do that. The words would be empty because they might not be able to save her father.

But they could save her.

"Keep talking, Ruby. What is going on in your restaurant?"

She chewed on her lip for a moment before the words started to spill out of her, tales of drugs being sold and shipments carried to Anchorage and farther to the lower forty-eight. With each word she spoke, Gasper saw some of the tension leave her body until she slumped in the chair, eyes red but no tears in sight.

"You did good, Ruby. Real good. Let's get you back to your restaurant."

Her head snapped up and she stared at Gasper with so much hope in her face that he knew she was still holding back with them and there was a lot more she wasn't saying.

"I'm going back?"

He nodded. "Penn, call the trooper in to uncuff her. She's coming with us."

Chapter Eight

Salty night wind rushed through White Fog, bringing the brine of the sea. Gasper leaned against the wall of the truck stop, staring into space, his mind churning like the water he couldn't see from here.

This mission felt even more tangled up than most. That bomber in the national forest and the people being killed by exploding packages seemed easy to solve compared to what was happening here.

But were they truly easier, or were they just easier to him? His feelings weren't involved then.

He'd taken things too far with her. He never should have laid a hand on her, let alone his mouth. His gut tightened at the memory of her sweet juices drenching his tongue as he licked her to completion.

When two of his brothers emerged from the convenience store armed with energy drinks and enough snacks to tide them over for the night, he pulled away from the wall to join them. Though he tuned into their conversation, his mind was back at Ruby's Place.

He and Penn had an in-depth discussion about whether or not to bug her with a listening device so they could detect what was going on with the Bratva and even get intel off those ugly bouncers. But in the end, the fact that the Russian mafia suspected everyone, even those who were loyal for years, had made them stop. Neither of them would put it past the bouncers to have apps on their phones that detected listening devices and hidden cameras.

So she was out there alone.

He and the guys crossed the parking lot and settled in the SUV. Some of the doors hung open and Broshears sat in the opening, sharpening the blade of his pocketknife.

Broshears cocked a brow at Winston. "You grab me my sunflower seeds?"

Winston reached into the bag he carried, found the seeds and tossed the bag to Broshears. He caught it out of the air and used his knife to slice into the bag.

Gasper leaned against the side of the SUV and gazed in the direction of Ruby's Place. What was she doing right now? Those assholes Big Mike and Max — Gasper learned they were really Maxim and Mikhail and wanted for evading arrest in their motherland — knew Ruby had been arrested. Were they questioning her right now? Using force?

He must have made a noise because every member of his team turned to him.

"What's goin' on, Gasper?"

"I don't like leaving her alone this long. I know the plan's to return at twenty-one hundred, but...I don't like it."

Nobody spoke for a moment. He caught Shadow exchanging a knowing look with Lipton.

Edgy already, Gasper jerked away from the side of the vehicle and planted his feet wide as he stared at his buddies. "What are you givin' each other that look for?"

Lipton's lips quirked at the corner. "Calm down, dude. You may be the jack-of-all-trades, but you've never experienced a situation like this, have you?"

"No," he almost growled.

"You're feeling confused. Overprotective to the point where you'd like to go in that restaurant and kill for her."

"Hell yeah!"

Shadow chuckled. "Man, you're learning a new skill."

He gaped at the special operative, waiting for him to expound on his statement. When he didn't immediately speak, he burst out, "Well?"

"You're learning what it is to care about a woman."

He closed his eyes, counted to ten and slowly reopened them to find half a dozen men shooting him grins or outright laughing at him.

He scowled at them. "Dicks."

They burst out in laughter. Gasper shook his head at their antics, which he'd also joined in on before when it came to the other team members falling in love.

Shit, was he? Falling in love? The strong word meant little to him, but if he dwelled on it, he only associated the emotion with seeing his mother's smiling face as she revealed his cake for his tenth birthday or his father slinging an arm around him when he got a home run in little league.

And he loved the men he fought alongside. That brotherhood came with a lot of emotions, but what he was feeling now for Ruby was different.

He'd hated seeing her in those handcuffs, fear dimming the lights of her beautiful eyes.

"Fuck you guys," he shot out, which earned him more laughter.

Finally, Penn spoke, and what he had to say ended their amusement. "I think Jack's right—we go in, order some drinks. Keep an eye on the woman."

His muscles clenched. "I'm ready."

"Man, you mean I don't get to eat my cupcakes?" Winston pulled a package from his bag.

Penn snorted with a chuckle of his own. "Nobody's stopping you from eating your cupcakes. Guys, I hope y'all have your singing voices tuned up, because we're going into Ruby's Place for karaoke."

This time Gasper laughed. "She claims they don't have karaoke, but we know Shadow's already tuning up to sing Elvis."

"I got the karaoke app on my phone." Shadow wasn't kidding.

They stowed their food and drinks inside the SUV, locked it up and took off walking in a group in the direction of the restaurant and bar. The wind flooded his nostrils with scent of the sea he'd grown used to during his time in Alaska. It was much different from his childhood home of Minnesota, where tree sap or the tang of crushed grass underfoot as he headed to the nearest lake for a spot of fishing flooded him with nostalgia.

Ruby had grown up here, though. This tiny speck on the map was her hometown. And it seemed most of the population lived under her roof.

Girls brought in by the mafia, they learned. Though she refused to say what happened to them after arrival, he could guess. He'd seen enough young girls trafficked to understand why she didn't want to speak of it.

After they settled at their usual long table and had drinks in hand, delivered by yet another girl nobody had ever seen before, Shadow stood up and announced to the room it was karaoke night and he was first on the list with "Love Me Tender."

As soon as he had the song up on his phone on high volume and hit his stride with the tune, Gasper spied the goon called Max striding toward the table.

140

He tensed. Penn was already dialed in to the bouncer.

When he got in Shadow's face, Gasper, Penn and Lipton moved as one. Gasper got Max around the neck, dragging him backward as Penn swiped his feet out from under him. Lipton had his hands pinned behind his back before the waitress got a full scream of alarm out.

The few patrons in the restaurant watched with interest but made no move to help the bouncer as they bundled him out of the restaurant.

"Hey! What are you doing!" The thump of feet on stairs sounded as they passed by the staircase carrying Max outside.

Ruby rolled to a stop at the foot of the stairs, took in the situation and surged toward them. "What are you doing?"

"Please stay back. We don't want you getting hurt."

She sucked in a sharp breath at Gasper's command. As they passed her carrying the man between them, a ruckus followed in the restaurant. By the sounds of it, Big Mike was riled by what they were doing to his friend, and the rest of the Xtreme Ops team had to put him in his place.

The Elvis tune cut short. Shit was going down with the other bouncer indoors.

Ruby issued a half scream of pure frustration and ran back inside.

Once they had the big man on the ground, with Lipton binding his hands with a zip-tie and Gasper's knee in his chest to pin him to the sidewalk, Penn rifled through his pockets and got his phone.

Now to bypass the lock screen. This wasn't their first rodeo, and Penn's skills were honed. In seconds, he bypassed the security code and accessed the device.

Again, they hadn't planned for this to happen, but the stars had aligned for them and put this man into their hands so they could see that app on his phone with the live footage of Ruby's father.

Max's chest vibrated with fury, and he spat a stream of curses tinged with his Russian accent.

Gasper glared down at the man. What harm had he done to Ruby? Did he grab her? Knock her around when she didn't do his bidding?

He was close to spouting all those accusations, but he checked himself in time. Penn swiped his finger over the phone screen before pocketing it.

"It's there?" Gasper asked.

"Yeah." He drew out his own phone and called the state trooper who'd assisted them earlier with Ruby. Having other law enforcement on their side always made things operate more smoothly.

Inside, a crash sounded. Seconds later, a couple who'd been enjoying a drink ran out. They spotted the bouncer pinned to the sidewalk and hightailed it from the restaurant. The night swallowed them.

"You guys got control here?" Penn asked.

"Go!" Gasper responded.

While Penn rushed back into the building to see what was happening, Gasper focused on Max's ugly face. He had the brow of a Neanderthal. His lips were thick and off-kilter too, like someone had smeared them across his face. And his beak of a nose had been broken more than once.

His chest heaved, and Gasper crushed his knee into his stomach deeper to hold him in place. The breath whooshed from him.

The door opened, casting a warm, gold glow over the sidewalk. The light crept toward where they had Max pinned, but it didn't illuminate them. The footsteps coming toward them didn't belong to any of the Xtreme Ops members.

Gasper glanced up to see Ruby. She balled her fists at her sides.

"Let him up!"

Gasper wished he could see her better to make out if she was playacting her outrage or she really was pissed that they'd thrown her bouncer out and turned the tables on him.

He wished they could just reach the root of the evil in residence here, but they just had to bide their time and wait for the men to come with another shipment of drugs, girls or both.

Then the mission would come to an end...and he wouldn't see Ruby again.

That didn't have to happen, he thought. He could stay in touch. Visit.

And what? Take her to bed and leave her with empty promises?

He swung his head to look away from her. "Ruby, go into the kitchen and wait for me."

He could almost hear her grinding her teeth. "Why should I obey you!"

"Go. Back. In. Please."

"Ugh!" She whipped around and stalked into the building.

Minutes later the state trooper who'd been waiting on standby showed up on the scene. The trooper arrested him for endangering the same minor Ruby had been arrested for earlier and he read him his rights. With the trooper's help, they bundled Max into the back of the car.

Gasper watched them drive off. Scraping a hand over his face, he muttered, "Fuck."

"Is that 'fuck, Ruby's pissed at me?'"

He dropped his head. "Hell yeah."

Lipton rested a hand on his shoulder. "Been there, brother. Go to her and I'll finish what the other guys started."

Gasper fisted his hands and a half-dozen knuckles popped. When he was old, he'd be so arthritic from his line of work.

As soon as he walked in, he saw Big Mike was nowhere to be seen. Had he already caught wind that his crony had been arrested and carted off to jail?

Penn waved Gasper over with barely a glance away from Max's confiscated phone. Damn. Ruby would have to wait.

He veered toward his captain. "What'd you find?"

He held out the phone to show him the man on the screen. Surrounded by the grungy gray walls of his prison cell, he lay curled on the bed, so still.

"Is he dead or sleeping?" he asked in a hushed voice.

"Dunno, but look close at his hand." Penn swiped a finger over the screen to zoom in on the twisted, broken digits. Something thin and white gleamed, and Gasper's stomach knotted.

"The bone's sticking out of the flesh."

Penn gave him a grave nod. "As soon as Broshears is done there" — he jerked his jaw toward the rest of the team who were back at the karaoke as a cover for their actions — "I'll set him to work tracing the feed. We need to find out where it's coming from."

Gasper nodded. "Ruby said Russia, but see that?" He pointed to the screen and the time stamp in the corner. Below it was a series of digits the Xtreme Ops team knew well.

The coordinates for Anchorage.

"Good catch, Jack. I didn't notice that. Guess we'll be sending half the team to Anchorage."

Gasper gave a nod. "Looks like operation find-the-father will soon be wrapped up. Next on the list: save the girls."

But first, another woman needed his attention.

Ruby heard Elias's heavy footsteps before she saw him. He appeared in the opening, huge and powerful and just about the only human she wanted to see right now, aside from her father.

When he set eyes on her, relief passed over his face. He took two steps into the kitchen, and she ran the rest of the distance. As soon as his strong arms enveloped her, she closed her eyes and drank in his manly scent.

"Why is this the only place I've felt safe in the past year?" She didn't mean to blurt it, but when Elias's arms tightened around her, she couldn't regret it. It felt too good.

He buried his face into her hair. "It means so much that you trust me, Ruby. Even after what I did today."

She shoved against his chest. "That's right! You disrupted my place of business. That B&B owner is always looking for a reason to bring the cops into my bar. Then! You got me arrested."

"And out of jail too." His lips tugged upward as he pulled her back into his arms.

She settled in his hold and took a moment to ground herself. She was alive. So was her father, for now. The girls were still all upstairs and unharmed. And now she had the backup of Elias and his men. Even though one bouncer was in jail and the other pissed off beyond measure.

"You claim you're special ops, but you have Navy tattoos."

"I can't explain yet. But I will, I promise."

She nodded, rubbing her cheek on his soft shirt. Underneath it, she felt a harder layer and realized he wore a bulletproof vest.

"Where have you guys been staying?" she asked.

"Around."

She couldn't think of any place in White Fog besides the B&B down the street. For years, the owner had nothing but bad things to say about Ruby's Place. Every man who hit his front steps became a suspect in his eyes, and she couldn't imagine he welcomed the special operatives into his establishment.

They must be sleeping in their vehicle. The thought of so many huge men piled on the seats like sleeping dogs made her shake her head.

He mistook her shaking her head as worry. "Trust me—we'll keep you safe."

"I want to trust you, but you don't know what you just did."

147

"We're aware. We've been dealing with these people for a while now. We have Max's phone, and we're analyzing it right now."

"Have you seen my father on the live cam?"

The grave way he nodded told her, her father's condition hadn't improved. A shallow sigh trickled out of her. She felt as twisted and wrung out as an old dishcloth. When would this end? How would she and her father get free? The mafia had long arms. They could find them anywhere.

"Ruby... Hell, do I even call you Ruby now?"

"Yes."

He cupped her face with all the tenderness she craved without realizing it. But a woman couldn't survive on working and worrying herself to the bone. "I just realized our first names are very close. Elliana and Elias."

"Oh God. We sound like some royal twins in a Disney movie."

His deep chuckle brought a smile to her face as well. Even if things ended badly, they had this millisecond of hope.

She moved onto tiptoe at the same moment he leaned down to kiss her. The soft crush of his lips on hers took away all her cares in a throbbing heartbeat. She lost herself to the increasing pressure of Elias's mouth and the swipe of his tongue through her mouth.

A soft shivery moan escaped her, and she clung to him. "I want you."

He grumbled with desire. "Shall I sweep you off to the laundry room?"

She searched his eyes. "No. C'mon." She pulled his hand, and he followed her through the kitchen to the hallway. Leading him past the laundry room and her office, she battled with her own feelings on having a man in her personal space.

Now, she drew her lover into her haven. He stopped to scan the space, and she watched his face display emotion after emotion as he took in the collection of everything that meant something to her.

He pointed to a photograph on the wall, black and white and in the original oval frame. "Your grandmother Ruby?"

She nodded.

"I see you in her."

A soft smile hit her lips.

Elias continued to examine her belongings, from the hand-me-down vanity with mirror where she seldom sat but had long ago become a place that caught all the junk she needed to put away and rarely did. Trinkets some of the girls had given her over the year she'd been their only link to normalcy in a new land—a tiny carved elephant, some rings with cheap but pretty stones and a necklace made of feathers, which Ruby didn't like but kept because of the thought behind it.

His attention landed on the bed, rumpled after she climbed from it and hastily dragged the covers over the mattress. An eclectic mix of pillows and blankets created something brightly colored.

He turned to her. "I love it."

"You don't have to say that because you want to get me between the sheets. You'll get that anyway."

His eyes warmed. Laying his palm along her cheek, he said, "No, really. I love it." Gently, he threaded his fingers into her hair, spanning them along her scalp. Her insides pitched and heaved like she stood aboard a ship out on the Bering Sea.

As he slid his other hand over her shoulder to cover her breast with his palm, her heart hiccupped and beat faster. Need sank low in her stomach. Something had changed between them. They were already lovers and coming back for more. But this time lust wasn't driving them.

Emotion was.

He'd offered her a ray of light in the dark world she lived in. He'd vowed to keep her safe from the clutches of the mafia. And the only wicked bone in his body was between his legs.

She gasped as he fondled her breast, closing his fingers over her nipple in a light pinch. She went for his shirt, yanking it up to find that bulletproof vest and a snug shirt she knew was beneath. Taking a moment to drink in how damn hot he looked in it, she felt his stare on her.

"It's still me." He took her hand and laid it on his chest. "Don't let it frighten you."

"I'm not frightened. I'm...turned on."

The air whooshed out of him. His chest heaved. In a quick move, he lifted her off her feet, slammed his mouth over hers and carried her to the bed. She wrapped her arms around him and angled closer to receive the deep passes of his tongue. Her pussy squeezed with raw desire, and a pulse took up in her core, deep in the place she wanted his fingers, tongue...cock.

With adept moves, he stripped off her clothes and then reached to his side to unbuckle the vest he wore. She plastered her hands over his warm, steely chest. Those tattoos he bore had alerted her to what he was, but she didn't care then, and she didn't now.

He was a warrior—her warrior.

She kissed him hard and deep, drawing moans from the man and giving them back. When he slipped his hand between her legs and cupped her pussy, she cried out. The heel of his hand pressed down on her clit. Her nerves snapped.

Slowly, he rubbed her, watching her face as she ignited at his touch. She rocked upward, rubbing back.

"Fuck yeah." He sank two fingers into her pussy. She bit back a scream. Fireworks shot off behind her eyes. Her body gripped at those fingers, but he withdrew them slowly, scissoring them apart to widen her for his entry soon.

"Oh God!" She clutched his shoulders.

"That's it, sweetheart. Hold on to me. Give yourself to me. God, do you know how beautiful you look right this minute?" His panting breaths matched hers.

He thrust his fingers deep, pulled out, plunged deeper. Curled his fingers and stroked her inner spot. Juices soaked him. And then he circled her clit with his thumb, over and over and over—

She came on a harsh cry. Her body pounded with the strong orgasm she hadn't totally expected. Need soared through her like a meteor, searing her with emotions.

Tears welled in her eyes. Seeing them, Elias leaned over her and tenderly brushed his lips to hers. "It's okay, sweetheart. You don't have to cry. I've got more where that came from."

An unexpected laugh burbled up.

Chapter Nine

Elias's hands shook as he slid the condom over his erection. God, this woman chained him in ways he didn't understand. It was as if she'd captured a piece of his soul and held it hostage.

Thing was...he didn't want it back.

He was falling for her, if he hadn't already. That foreign little four-letter word performed backflips through his mind. When he braced his arms on each side of her and drove his cock into her tight sheath, the declaration threatened to burst from his lips.

"Elias!" She rocked against him, taking as well as giving. Her bright hair spilled in waves over the colorful, patterned cover of her bed. Her room looked like a gypsy caravan, a mix of patterns and colors that should clash but instead worked. They were pure Ruby.

Her eyes blazed up at him. The depths held passion and more...so much more. Did she feel it too? He wasn't alone in this, was he?

Planting his hand on her ass, he pulled her up and into him, sinking his cock into her heated walls.

She sucked on his neck and found his ear. With both hands bracketing his face, she kissed him with a fierce need that spiked his own. His balls throbbed. That tingle at the base of his spine threatened that he could blow too soon. No matter if he did—he'd roll with it and eat her pussy until she came several more times.

He loved watching her too much. Couldn't get enough. Would he ever?

As he swung his hips back and then thrust into her again, she gripped him hard. One look at her expression told him she was on the edge. About to...

She squeezed the hell out of him. Her walls tightened, clamped and sucked at him. He didn't have a prayer of staving off that release now. Arching, he issued a roar of completion.

Three spurts, then four and five... He collapsed on the sixth and damn near died on the seventh. No woman had ever pulled that much from him. Whatever hold she had on him extended clear to his cock.

He grinned down at her and kissed her. Stunned, she didn't immediately kiss him back but when she did, he felt the joy rising inside her like a tide. At long last, he pulled the emotion from her that he'd wanted from the start. Making her happy was quickly becoming his main goal. Right up there with keeping her safe and stopping the fucking mafia from terrorizing her, her father and all those women upstairs.

She flipped her tongue against his. He groaned and rolled with her, settling her atop him. Her weight felt perfect. He could lie here forever.

Fuck. Forever couldn't last more than a few stolen moments — his team needed him. Penn could be looking for him now.

Ruby nuzzled his neck. "Don't get up yet. Don't go. Stay here with me."

How did a man withstand a plea like that?

They didn't have long together, but he wanted to make the most of it. Warmth spread through his chest, layer upon layer.

Untangling himself from this knot wouldn't be easy — it wasn't only his libido or a Superman complex. He didn't know what to call it, but it was much deeper. He'd broken the rules and now someone would pay the price. Without hesitation, he knew he'd bear the brunt of any ramifications.

Then he glanced up and saw Ruby's eyes shining up at him.

Hell, he could free her from the mafia…but getting her free of him would be a lot more difficult.

He gently eased her off him and swung his legs out of bed. "I have to go. The guys will be waiting for me."

She sat up and held a fat pillow over her nakedness. The little white pompoms on the pillow only made the woman behind it look more enticing.

155

His cock started to throb again as he disposed of the condom and dressed.

"Elias, what's going to happen?" Her voice held a quaver.

He tugged his shirt down and leaned over the bed to press a kiss between her furrowed red brows. "I don't want you to worry about the bouncers. We'll take care of them."

"That's what I'm afraid of. Their bosses—"

With a fingertip beneath her chin, he drew her face up to meet his eyes. "We'll handle them too, sweetheart. Trust us."

She didn't relax and continued to wear a scowl. "What am I supposed to do while you're off 'handling' everything?"

"Business as usual. You run your business the same way you always do. Don't do anything different because that's what will raise alarms with the Bratva."

She blew out a breath, which caused a tendril of red hair to float away from her face. "Fine. Just understand that you might not like the way I run my business."

He threw her an amused glance. "You've survived for this long by making tough decisions. Even though you're now working with us, I know you'll do great." He brushed his lips across her brow again. She tipped her head up, and he pressed a kiss to her lips too.

It was wrenching, but he left the sexiest woman alive naked in her bed to join up with his team. He found Penn and Broshears in the restaurant, heads together, speaking quietly. The customers and the rest of the Xtreme Ops team were gone. There was no sign of Big Mike either.

"You send the other bouncer with the state police too?" he asked as he neared the guys.

Penn grunted. "Nothing so perfect as that. He's pissed with the cops who arrested his buddy, and the Bratva won't be happy about it either, but they can't make a move without blowing their cover."

"Yeah, he'll either shut up and live with it or shake some trees."

"Somethin' along those lines. Your woman okay?"

Gasper inflated his chest with a huge gulp of air. "Yes, she's holding up."

He knew she was also drenched from the orgasms he'd given her. A vision of her pale skin hidden behind the pillow filled his brain. He pushed the image to the recesses of his mind and focused on his duty.

"So the dude is tattling to the Bratva right now. Think they're going to show up here to defend their stronghold?" Gasper swiped his hand over his face and caught a hint of Ruby's scent on his fingers.

"It's the move we need right now, Jack. Shadow is hacking the bouncer's phone. I've got Beckett,

157

Winston and Day searching for the location of Ruby's father."

"The rest of the team?"

"Staked out around the perimeter right now." He lifted his jaw to gesture to their location.

"What can I do?" Gasper stood at attention, awaiting his order.

"I'd like you to speak with the young woman who turned Ruby in. See what you can find out."

"Where is she?"

"The B&B owner down the street took pity on her and put her up in a room. You can find her there. Report back as soon as you're finished."

Gasper gave a nod and set off immediately for the bed and breakfast. The outside of the building was simple, with a peaked metal roof to withstand the snowy Alaskan winters. The front porch boasted a few cheap lawn chairs and a table where a visitor could set a drink. It wasn't exactly five-star, but it served a purpose here in White Fog.

When he rapped on the door, the owner grumbled at the sight of him. "I told you guys I don't have rooms for you." He started to shut the door in his face, and Gasper wedged the toe of his boot in it.

"I need to see a guest who's staying here."

"This isn't that kind of establishment. Go to Ruby's Place if you're looking for that!" He started to smash the door against Gasper's boot.

In a quick step, he shoved his way into the B&B. The man stepped back, anger reddening his face.

"You can either tell me where to find the woman — or fetch her here for me — or I'll go looking for her myself." He pointed to a chair in front of the simple stone fireplace. "I'll wait right here."

The man's anger faded to a spark, and he muttered under his breath. Gasper couldn't make out the words, but a second later, the woman appeared in the room.

Gasper stood from the chair. "Hello."

She stared at him. The owner stood behind him, smiling. For what reason?

"I'd like to talk to you about what you told the police about being kicked out of Ruby's Place."

She blinked at him, and all at once he realized she spoke little if no English. Quickly, he repeated himself in Russian, and the owner's eyes bulged out.

"Leave us," Gasper commanded him in English. The man hurried off. He could eavesdrop, but he probably wouldn't understand a word they exchanged, so Gasper didn't follow him.

"Sit down please," he told the woman in her native tongue. Or at least he assumed it to be — she hadn't given any indication she knew Russian either.

Then, very hesitantly, she crossed the room and sank to a chair. So, he had gotten through to her.

"How did you come to be here?"

"By boat," she answered after a long pause.

"Who brought you?"

She pressed her lips into a line. She was protecting the men who intended to sell her before she was evicted from Ruby's Place for doing drugs.

"The men who brought you here can't hurt you. You're under my protection. Do you know their names?"

She shook her head.

"What port did you sail from?"

On and on the questioning went, with her answering in short monosyllables at times. When he brought up Ruby, the woman lifted her jaw in defiance and her eyes snapped with fury.

"She kicked me out. She had no right to do that."

"She says it's her rule that you're not allowed to do drugs."

"What was I supposed to do—tell the man I was with no? He paid good money for me, and if he wanted me to take drugs, I had no choice."

Gasper's chest burned. No, her choices had been taken from her in Russia when she was given the false promise of a better life. Only she'd arrived here to prostitute herself until the time she'd be moved from Ruby's Place, on her way to marry the highest bidder.

"You have a choice now," he told her. "Do you want to go home or apply for a green card and work in the US?"

"I have nothing in Russia. It's why I came here. But Ruby ruined my life by kicking me out. Now I'll never marry a rich man."

So the girls were promised rich husbands and wonderful bounty if they boarded the ship. Gasper had seen too many cases like this and knew better. They ended up abused, beaten, on the streets or on the news as a crime victim.

He went to the entry and looked around. The owner was nowhere to be seen, but as soon as Gasper called for him, he appeared.

"I'm going to pay for her stay here. I'll return in the morning with money."

He narrowed his eyes. "No funny business. If you want to keep a woman for your pleasure, go to R—"

"I know, I know," he cut the man off. "Go to Ruby's Place." He was sick of hearing the name of the woman he cared for besmirched. "If you can make sure she doesn't leave with anyone, I'll pay double the room rate."

The owner stared at him. Gasper saw the moment greed overcame any animosity he had toward the Xtreme Ops team or the goings-on down the street.

"Deal."

Gasper clasped his hand hard enough that the man winced. He didn't usually take pleasure in cowing innocent men, but this one made it clear he was no friend. Besides, he had to keep up his end of the bargain to protect the woman.

As he left the establishment, he played through his conversation with the girl. Had he learned anything from her? Nothing more than they already knew — that the mafia would go to any extreme for more power and money.

If it was the last thing he ever did, he would get Ruby free of them.

Ruby scrubbed at the table surface so hard that she wouldn't be surprised to lift the cloth and see the finish rubbed away. To say she was pissed off at her life right now was the understatement of the century.

As if having her father held prisoner or the Russian mafia questioning her every move wasn't enough pressure, now she was a freakin' informant for a branch of the government she'd never even heard about. She wouldn't have bought the story of a homeland security special ops unit if the captain hadn't shown her proof at the police barracks.

But that was the least of her worries. The Bratva allowed her enough control to make a no-drug rule, but they frowned upon her kicking out the girls that made them big bucks. Not to mention that her bouncer had been arrested. How long before the Bratva invaded Ruby's Place and showed her who really held the power? As if she wasn't totally, painfully aware.

She finished scrubbing one table and moved to the next.

Usually she relished this time of night when she was done serving food and drinks. The place still held the magic of her grandmother, but she only saw that when she could commune with the space in silence.

The walls bore pictures collected over the years. Local scenery and groups of fishermen. Big nets and huge catches of the day spilled out over the deck of some ship. A few of them, she recalled the moments, such as a huge snowstorm that had dropped so many feet on White Fog that she wasn't allowed outside for days because the snow was up over her head.

One thing interrupted her after-hours solace, and that was the telltale knock of the male visitors. The mafia sent men here to slake their needs, and the girls upstairs accommodated. The fact they believed they must sell their bodies in trade for a new life cut her to the soul. What could she do but try to protect them?

She'd only been protecting the other girls when she threw Jenicka out of the house for doing drugs. She'd seen it early on—one girl got roped into snorting coke or shooting heroin and pretty soon she had a whole house full of pretty, strung-out zombies.

It hurt her to toss girls out, but she couldn't compromise herself—or her father.

He felt farther from her every day. Seeing him on the screen beaten and battered sliced her like a knife. But after so much time had passed, she started to lock those feelings in a box, one only pried opened when

163

Big Mike or Max reminded her of why she was doing this.

Working off a debt.

The rest of her life was a daily grind. Fatigue, burnout and having little to fill up her soul.

Then Elias walked through the door.

Upon first sight, she felt a pull to the man. It wasn't only lust or his rugged good looks, either. She'd fought it. And given in. Let herself feel…and hope.

That was the scariest part. In her lifetime, she'd learned that *hope* was the ugliest four-letter word in the human language. It could—would—be crushed.

Those stolen moments when Elias had pleasured her and given her tender looks had done more to lift her spirits than anything in her life. With him, she felt renewed and able to keep trudging up her arduous, rocky path.

A light tapping noise made her freeze mid-swipe over the table.

She abandoned her task and hurried through the kitchen to let him in.

She didn't know his name, but he was a truck driver who came into town every three days or so, carrying loads of fish and crab to be sold in other parts of Alaska. Every time he showed up, he requested Polina.

"Come in."

He tugged at the bill of his broken-in hat. "I was hoping Polina would be available tonight."

Ruby nodded. "She's up in her room. You remember the way."

He slipped a handful of bills to Ruby. She tucked these in her apron and returned to scrubbing tables. She didn't finish the first one when she heard footsteps on the stairs again.

She glanced up to see the man coming down. "Polina isn't there."

Shock hit her. Not there? What did he mean? She rushed past him and took the stairs at a fast pace, reaching the top in seconds. She strode straight to Polina's room. Some of the other women shared rooms, because they were so filled up, but not Polina.

She didn't bother to knock and threw it open wide.

Fucking hell, he's right.

She ran to the top of the stairs and called down to the man, "Next visit's on the house. Get out."

Then she scurried to the first bedroom. Down the line on each side of the hallway, she knocked loudly. Girls started to appear, half-asleep and in various states of undress. One had a man in her bed, and she'd twisted the sheet around her body, but her lips were swollen, and she wore a bite mark on her shoulder.

"I need a head count! Start counting off!"

Ruby's mind whirled as she wondered what could have happened to Polina. No men had come for her today, so she couldn't have been taken. She might have run off, though. Who could blame her? Living in a room, giving her body or cleaning bathrooms to earn her keep. The dreams she'd arrived in America with were crushed long ago.

The final number reached Ruby's ears. "One is missing."

"Who is it?" Anushka asked.

"Polina. Has anyone seen her?"

Several girls shook their heads, and a few answered with no.

"Go back to bed." She pointed to the girl with the bite on her shoulder. "You — don't let him hurt you. If he does, you kick him in the balls and throw him out. Understand? You're strong."

She nodded, a new gleam in her eye that left Ruby with no question as to how long that man would remain in her bed.

Hurrying downstairs again, Ruby made a quick search of the place. Polina hadn't made a midnight snack run to the kitchen, and she wasn't out in the garden either. She wasn't here.

Heart racing, she snatched her phone from her jeans pocket and dialed the only person she knew could help her — Elias.

He picked up immediately.

"There's a girl missing," she announced without preamble.

"We know."

Her jaw dropped, and she stared blindly in terror at her surroundings. "You know?"

"Yes."

What had they done? Were they trying to get her father killed? Or her? Anger hit, with the team claiming to help her and also aimed at herself. She never should have gotten involved with them. They were nothing but trouble, and their goal wasn't her goal.

She found her voice, but it sounded like sandpaper. "You have no idea…what you've done."

Too angry to go on, she hung up on Elias.

She shoved the phone in her pocket and started to turn. Something struck her cheek—hard. Stunned, she stumbled back. Had she walked into an open cupboard door?

Another blow threw her across the room. Warm, sticky blood trickled from her lip.

Her mind reeled in pain and shock. She had to push her legs under her and push herself up off the floor. Oh God—the Bratva had found out everything and were in her kitchen, weren't they? Cool tile underneath her palms grounded her. She tipped her head back and peered around.

The man standing in front of her, legs braced wide and a snarl on his lips, was very familiar. Mikhail.

"Big Mike—" she started.

"Shut up!" he commanded in a booming voice. "You lost a woman, and that's worth more than a beating from the men who own you and your weak father."

Pain radiated through her cheek and eye as the bruising pooled beneath the skin from Big Mike's massive dinner-plate sized hand. He wore knuckle rings too, and one had cut her skin on the second blow.

Her insides shrank as she processed what he was saying. "She ran off. We have to go find her."

He glared at her. "Do you really believe that?"

She nodded.

But did she? Not after what Elias said.

They knew Polina left, and they knew where she was. Had they taken her? Or somehow persuaded her to become another informant?

The special operatives might think they were trying to help her, but the truth was they'd made things so much worse.

"Mikhail. Please stop. I'll find out where she is. Just…give me time."

"Do you think your father has time?"

Panic was hard to feel these days. After threatening her with killing her father so many times, her body had stopped feeling it so keenly. But this time she did — right down to her toes.

She shoved to her feet and swayed. Catching hold of the counter, she attempted to steady herself. A trickle of warmth down her cheek reminded her that his ring had cut her.

With nothing left inside her but her iron will, she met Big Mike's eyes. "I will get Polina back."

He stared at her for a moment that was weighted with the promise of violence. "The rest of the girls go as soon as I can arrange it."

He turned to lumber out of the kitchen. She watched him go, holding her tears at bay. She wasn't a crier, and over the past year she'd been drowning in this mess, she had almost forgotten how to. But a single tear slipped from the corner of her eye.

She let it slide down her face and drop from her jaw. Then she shut down the waterworks. That was all the pity she'd allow herself because she had too much to do.

First on the list, find Elias and kick his ass. Damn those guys for screwing everything up. He told her to trust him, but how could she? He only saw the situation from his own angle, not hers. *His* father wasn't being held prisoner. The women entrusted to her and who she'd vowed to protect didn't matter as much to him.

She needed to find Polina, as well as worry about when the Russians would sell off the women under her roof. Her face hurt like hell, and the bruising sent throbs of pain to her skull.

If she didn't take care of herself first, what good would she be to anyone else in her care?

She walked to the cupboard and pulled out a bottle of painkillers. She took two and then moved to the freezer for an ice pack. Last and most important to her self-care, she walked out to the bar and poured herself a drink. In the silence and darkness, she hoped the alcohol burned away some of her fear, because she had a lot to do.

Gasper's hands shook, and they never shook. He was rock solid every second of his life.

Except this one.

Ruby was in trouble—he knew it from the edge in her voice on the phone. More than anger infused her tone, and he had to reach her—now, before something bad happened.

He scrubbed a hand over his face to gain a grip on himself before making the request to his captain to go to her. What he feared most was Penn telling him no. Gasper didn't know what would happen then.

Lungs burning, muscles stiff, he stalked over to his captain. "Permission to go to Ruby's Place, sir."

Penn eyed him. "Denied."

"Denied?" His voice came out low and deadly.

Hearing it, his captain squared up with him. "Yes, denied," he barked.

"Permission to speak freely."

"Not granted. We need you to take the woman to the safehouse. There isn't time."

Penn was a hard man, but he was fair. He had the ability to see a situation from several angles, which was what made him such a good leader. So why was he being such a hard-ass right now? And on this matter?

"Captain, Ruby just called. She's going to get in trouble for that girl leaving." When Broshears had cornered Polina and convinced her to come with them and they'd keep her safe, Gasper hadn't been in on it until it was too late, and the girl left.

He fisted his hands when Penn gave him a long look that told him that his orders would be followed, or Gasper wouldn't like the consequences.

"Goddammit, Penn! Listen to me!"

An arm banded around his chest and dragged him off a few feet, out of swinging distance. Gasper wasn't so far gone as to throw a punch at his captain, but it was damn close. Why? He had to reach Ruby, that was why.

"Let me go! Shadow, goddammit! Penn, you know how this feels! You feel the same for Cora!"

His buddy's grip didn't ease up as he hauled him several more feet away. "Get hold of yourself, man!"

"He knows what the mafia will do to her if they find out she lost a woman! They'll kill her father. Kill her!" His rough tone ended on a rasp, and across the room, Penn gave him a long look.

Gasper continued to fight. "Let me go to her! I need to make sure she's safe. Another man can take the woman to the safehouse. It doesn't need to be me." He struggled free of Shadow's hold and stormed up to his captain.

He gave him a pointed look. "I have to go to her."

"You're too fucking close to this, Jack."

He shook his head. "This isn't a matter of close. It's protecting our informant. We can guard the perimeter of the building, but that doesn't mean we can see what's happening inside. That bouncer's still in there with her. Men are coming and going all night long. Who's to say one isn't the Bratva coming with an order to take her out?"

He didn't want to even think the damn words, but they were out now, and truth rang in the air.

Penn scrubbed a hand over his head and down his face as if something he'd said finally hit home. Maybe when he brought up Cora. "Fine. Go. Keep me informed."

"Thank you, sir. I'm sorry, sir."

He ran the entire distance to Ruby's Place, breath puffing and his head whirling with the possible ramifications for his actions. Had he fought so hard because of a gut instinct or did he really just need to

172

see with his own eyes that the woman he cared about was safe?

Gasper didn't often have to use his skill of lock-picking, but it was like riding a bike. The minute he flicked upward on the inner workings, it clicked open. He pocketed the metal tool and entered Ruby's Place through the kitchen.

A light had been left on over the sink, but shadows swallowed every corner. On edge, he searched the rooms off the kitchen too. At Ruby's room, he paused. Walking in on a woman as tough as Ruby when she was asleep could spell disaster for him. He wouldn't put it past her to sleep with a weapon beneath her pillow.

The fact she had to ward off thugs like those bouncers burned through him, leaving his hands shaking with fury.

He clasped Ruby's bedroom door handle and gently pushed it inward. Luckily, it didn't creak, but that didn't matter in the end because she wasn't in there.

Where was she?

Since the bathroom stood open and showed him she wasn't there either, he continued toward the restaurant and bar.

The dark space drew him in. He felt her presence like a wild animal can sense water.

He could creep as silently as a predator, yet he wanted to make her aware he'd come.

She looked up at the sound of his boots on the floor. When she turned her head, he saw she held something against her cheek.

He lunged forward. "Christ, are you hurt?" He reached her in a few long strides and dropped to his knees. Lifting his hand toward her cheek, he searched her face.

Ice—she was holding ice to her face.

White rage shot through his system as he tenderly guided her hand and the ice pack away from her cheek. The delicate curve was swollen, and a bruise darkened beneath her pale skin, apparent even in the darkness of the room.

She was cut too.

"Who did this to you?" His fury was barely banked in his tone.

Her stormy eyes lit on his. "You're shaking."

Not aware until this moment that he was letting his emotions get the better of him, he slammed them into a vault and locked it. He couldn't be weak— Ruby needed him. His team relied on him.

"You can't let them get to you too, Elias," she whispered.

So he was right about his earlier thought that she was looking out for him. Throwing up a shield between him and those bouncers in order to keep them from trying to rip his head off… At the same time she had to keep peace with the assholes, didn't she? How much longer did her father have? Days? Hours? He might already be dead.

He glided to his feet and drew her up with him. Though his instinct was to pick her up and keep on walking, he simply took her hand and led her to her bedroom.

She came with him, her fingers chilled in his grasp and infuriating him even more. He hadn't protected her. He was going to kill whoever hurt her.

In her room, he lit the lamp on the bedside table and made her sit on the mattress. Once again, he knelt before her to examine her face. "Who did this to you?"

She didn't respond, lips sealed into a pale line.

"You know I'll find out."

"It's just a bruise."

Looking at her, he didn't buy that bullshit for a minute. Pain and fear swirled in the depths of her eyes. A noise erupted from him, rough and grating, and he swooped to his feet, sat on the bed and pulled her into his lap.

She didn't fight him and curled against his chest. He dragged in a deep breath of her scent. He was falling in love with her. All signs pointed to the fact he wouldn't be able to walk away from her ever again.

"Let me get you out of here," he pleaded quietly.

"No. Just hold me tonight, Elias." She tipped her face up, and he lost himself in a whirlwind of feelings that tightened his chest and set him free all at the same time.

Tenderly, he guided a lock of red hair off her cheek to look closely at the injury. "I'm sorry I wasn't here to protect you."

She lay her palm over his heart. "I know you're doing what you feel is right. I can't argue with that since I do the same thing with my business. Besides...you're here now."

In a smooth maneuver, he lay her on the bed and stretched out beside her. His body reacted to her curves, cock already growing hard, but he didn't come here for sex.

She had other ideas, though. She leaned in and kissed him. The soft brush of her mouth drove him crazy, but he held completely still while she explored his lips and touched her tongue to his.

A growl rumbled in his chest. As passion took hold of them both, she threw herself atop him, and he grabbed her ass. She rocked into his erection, silently begging with her mouth in harsh sweeping kisses.

She needed comfort, and he had everything to give.

They stripped each other. She latched on to his neck and then drew a path of kisses down to his chest. Each warm flick of her tongue across his skin ignited something far deeper than lust.

Threading his fingers into her hair, he watched her move down his body and envelop his cock in her sweet mouth. Need roared in his ears. His balls tightened to his body and precum leaked from the tip of his cock to wet her tongue.

"Fuck, sweetheart. I can't last."

She met his stare, her mouth full of his cock. He almost lost it on the spot, but he held back somehow as she pulled off him. "I want to pleasure you," she whispered.

"You do. God, you do." He took control, rolling her gently into the covers and sliding down her body, kissing, licking and teasing her skin with kisses all the way to the *V* of her thighs.

She cried out when he covered her slit with his open mouth. She bucked, and he slipped the point of his tongue into her tight cavern. Delicious juices hit his tastebuds, and he groaned for more. Cupping her ass, he feasted on her drenched hole and folds. When he reached her clit and lapped at the bundle of nerves, she cried out and came.

All the missions in the world didn't compare to this moment with this woman. The light of his life.

The love of his life.

He laved her with his tongue, bringing her down from her high. When he moved up her body with his cock poised to enter her, she met his stare.

She grasped his cock at the root and guided it toward her pussy, granting permission to take her with no barriers.

Why did he feel like it was a claiming?

In one shove, he filled her pussy. Her mouth popped open on a gasp, and he thrust his tongue inside. She wrapped her arms and legs around him, riding his cock and driving him to the point of no return.

Her insides clamped on his length.

"Come with me. Now, Ruby!" He lost it first, the first spurt hitting her bare walls. He had no cares whether they made a child, because he'd take care of them both for the rest of his days. He'd live for them alone.

A roar bottled in his throat, but he held it in, groaning through his orgasm and rocking hard and fast while she shattered too.

Their kiss spiraled on for long minutes after completion, and she ended up in his arms where she belonged.

"Ruby…" Did he confess his love for her? A woman like her would more than likely run. Besides, until he knew what promises he could even offer, there was no point in saying them.

She met his stare, her eyes deep pools of tumult. Did she feel anything for him in return?

He didn't speak what was in his heart. He cupped the unbruised side of her face. "Did I hurt you at all?" he murmured.

She shook her head and covered his hand with hers. "No. You can't hurt me, Elias. We both know that."

Chapter Ten

"How did a nice girl like you get mixed up in this?"

Ruby snuggled closer to Elias's chest. The pleasant aftershocks of an amazing orgasm coupled with feeling safe after what happened in the kitchen with Big Mike left her feeling boneless.

"I've never told anybody this, but…my grandmother, the original Ruby, ran a brothel. Everyone knew and no one ever told."

"Did you know growing up?"

"I knew she let young women board here. I saw men coming and going, but this is a fisherman's town. And women are scarcer than men in Alaska."

The brush of his fingertips over her spine lifted the tiny hairs on her body, and she stretched like a cat for more. What was it about this man? He was different.

She'd think on that later, though. For now, he wanted the story.

"After my grandmother passed, my father took over, but he spent most of his time in the bar instead of the kitchen. He started running poker games out of here and ended up in deep with the Bratva."

"Unfortunately, it's an age-old story I've heard many times before."

She nodded. Her throat was suddenly thick, and she swallowed hard to dispel a lump. "I hate it here. I never wanted this life, but I have to work off my father's debt before I can leave."

He fell silent, but Elias was one of those men who was always energized. She felt his muscles humming under her body and could practically hear his mind ticking. When she lifted her head and looked at him, he winced.

"What is it?" she asked.

"You have one hell of a shiner." He skimmed his fingers over her brow while staring at her cheek.

"Just what I need." Big Mike would be puffing out his chest that he'd done this to her. She'd seen what kind of man he was too many times.

"Was it that asshole you call Big Mike?" A tendon in the crease of Elias's jaw seemed to pulsate, and she heard the creak of his molars.

"I don't want to talk about it. Please don't stir up more trouble than you already have." She sat up and drew the sheet over her breasts. "What *did* happen to Polina? What did you do?"

He scooted into a seated position with his spine propped against the pillows. "She's safe. That's all I can tell you for now."

She arched a brow at him.

"If someone pressures you, they can force you to tell them what you know about her, Ruby. It's better if you know nothing."

Okay, she saw his point — didn't mean she liked it.

She started to tell him as much, but a crash sounded in the front of the building.

Leaping from the bed, she reached for the first garment she saw, which was a thick robe. She shoved her arms into it as she ran from the room. Elias was only steps behind her.

She whirled to him, hand out to stop him in his tracks. "Stay here. Nobody knows you're in here, and I need to keep it that way!"

His eyes narrowed on her face. "I won't leave you unprotected again."

"I'm fine! Stay here. I'll call you if I need you." With that, she took off through the hall and pushed on the kitchen door to send it swinging. When her bare feet hit the wood floors of the restaurant, she spotted several girls grouped at the bottom of the stairs.

Ruby rushed over. "What happened?"

"Alina fell."

Pushing her way closer to the group, she assessed the brunette on the floor holding her ankle. "Is it broken?"

She shook her head and in rapid Russian, spouted off that she thought her ankle was merely twisted. Ruby helped her up, and with another girl supporting Alina on the other side, they helped her to a chair. She sank to it and moaned in pain.

Ruby looked to her go-to girl. "Anushka, call the mobile health unit and see if they're in one of the nearby villages so Alina can be examined."

Anushka hurried to do her bidding, and Ruby bent to look closer at Alina's ankle. It was puffing up.

"How did you fall?" she asked her.

"I was in a hurry to tell you that Marta is gone!"

Ruby's blood turned to ice like the shore of White Fog in January. "Gone?"

Alina nodded. "We share a room, so I'd know."

"Are her belongings gone?"

She nodded and bit her lip as tears filled her blue eyes.

"Son of a bitch!" Ruby rocketed to her feet and took off upstairs to see for herself. After a quick sweep of the room the girls shared, she ran down again at breakneck speed.

She gave rapid orders to elevate Alina's foot and to ice it until they heard from the health unit. Since White Fog was so small, there wasn't a resident doctor, and a mobile clinic traveled the area, making rounds from small village to village. Who knew when the next time they'd show up on the single street of White Fog?

182

The alternative was to drive the girl to a bigger town with a hospital and pray Ruby could dodge questions about the girl who didn't speak a lick of English. No—she had to hope the clinic showed up here or tend to the injury using the knowledge she had acquired over the years.

First, she needed to speak to the man hiding in her room. Curse those guys for ever coming here!

When she threw open her bedroom door, Elias was on his feet, fully dressed, waiting for her.

"What happened? I don't like not being in the action."

She hurled the door shut, and the perfume bottles on her dresser shook from the force of the slam. She faced him, hands on hips to keep them from shaking with anger. "A second girl's gone missing! Why do I have a feeling you know where she is?"

"Goddammit." He sliced his fingers through his hair and moved toward her.

She sidestepped him to avoid touching him. She couldn't trust her body to obey her command to stay away from the man—she wanted him too much.

"What did you do, Elias?" she hissed furiously.

"I—"

She cut him off, hand raised. "I know—you can't say. Well, I can't say I need you here anymore. All you're doing is causing me trouble!" She ignored the way his expression blanked as if he'd severed any emotions he had.

"Wait. Take this." He thrust a slip of paper into her hand. "Memorize it and then throw it out. You can reach me without being traced. Remember this if you need me."

She crushed the paper in her hand, grabbed some clothes and stormed away, intending to dress in the bathroom across the hall. "You can see yourself out!"

As Gasper approached, the knot of men grouped at the SUV broke apart and looked at him. Each stride he took felt loaded with all the frustration and power he couldn't do anything with.

What happened to this being an in-and-out job? They were fucking around too long. They knew where the girls were and had the means to stop the Bratva. He didn't understand why the clock had stopped ticking on this mission, but now at the worst possible time, they were pulling the girls out of Ruby's Place?

Shadow stepped out of the concealment of darkness, just as his name implied. He paused at Gasper's expression. "What the hell happened?"

"We can't take any more girls. It's putting Ruby in too much danger."

Penn faced him. "Fill us in."

"That fucking bouncer hit her because a girl went missing."

"Fuck," Penn bit out.

Gasper's fists clenched involuntarily at the thought of that asshole laying hands on her again. Even if she was angry with Elias – or never wanted to see him again – she still had his protection.

"Our plan to get the girls out safe before shit really goes down isn't the plan anymore," he said.

"You're right. If we get anyone out, it has to be that big dude Mikhail."

Several of the team nodded at Penn's statement.

Shadow brought his hand down on Gasper's shoulder and squeezed. "This is my doing. If I hadn't seen that girl out walking and convinced her to leave Ruby's Place, this wouldn't have happened."

Gasper bowed his head. "You did what you believed to be correct in the moment. She is better off protected by us than prostituting herself until she's sold to a 'husband' later."

Penn glanced at the phone in his hand and then brought it to his ear. "Captain Sullivan."

He listened for a moment, his jaw tightening. He turned to stare toward the road leading to the few buildings that made up White Fog. "Hell," he grated out. "We'll be there in five."

Every man went on high alert, prepared to grab weapons and dig in for war.

Penn swept his gaze over the group. "The guy who runs the B&B was just found dead."

"Jesus Christ. And the first girl Ruby kicked out – Jenicka? Is she still there?"

"That's undetermined."

"If the Bratva showed up there to take her, and the B&B owner got in the way..." Shadow drifted off, but he didn't need to continue. They all knew what he was thinking, and he was probably correct.

Gasper checked his sidearm. "Ready to roll, Captain."

Penn shot him an odd look before he gave a nod. That look left Gasper wondering what he wanted to say to him but held back. After their disagreement, they needed to clear the air. There wasn't time now.

A minute later, they were speeding toward the bed and breakfast. On the short drive, Penn shared the details. The state police received a call from an anonymous woman saying the owner was dead on the floor in the kitchen.

"Could that anonymous woman be Jenicka?" Gasper asked.

"Unlikely—she doesn't speak English, right? She didn't say the cause of death, but we're about to find out." Penn parked and the team didn't bother hiding who they were to any nosy people of White Fog as they piled out and rushed the building.

Gasper, Shadow and Winston took the back. Gasper glanced at the muddy spots of the garden for footprints as he closed in. Seeing nothing more than a few canine paw prints and a crushed flower or two, he reached the house with Shadow in the lead.

"Don't touch anything," Penn's voice projected into everyone's comms devices.

Gasper's team made certain the place was clear of danger before they reached the kitchen and found the dead man. Sure enough, he was sprawled there, facedown.

"Looks like he was making an escape," Gasper commented.

Winston crouched beside the body. A small pool of blood seeped from beneath him. "Shot in the back."

Calls of "clear" and "all clear" filled Gasper's ear, and then Penn and Lipton appeared while the rest of the team checked on the people staying upstairs. One of them would get Jenicka out and question her about the matter.

Gasper directed his stare from the body. "Goddammit. My guess is the Bratva knows that the girl's been staying here and came after him."

"Lip, increase the security around the other girls we took just in case," Penn said.

"What about Ruby?" Gasper blurted out.

Penn met his stare when he gave Lipton the command, "Get some eyes on Ruby's Place too. As usual, we're spread too thin, even in a town this small."

Again, Gasper got the feeling Penn wasn't stating everything he wanted to.

"You might as well say whatever it is you're holding back."

All the men looked up at him.

Penn never threw punches without landing on his target, and he didn't now. "All right. I wanted to get you alone, but we'll do this now. You're too close on this mission, Jack. We need you to take about ten steps away from your feelings for Ruby, or step down from it altogether."

"Step down from it altogether," he repeated dully. His chest burned. "My feelings aren't in play here. I'm protecting our informant!"

"Yes, and you're correct. But you can't stand there and tell me that if Ruby's life was at risk that you wouldn't put your teammates in danger to save her."

Gasper went dead and cold inside. He loved his brothers. Would do anything to save them, including taking a bullet for them. But he'd do the same for Ruby, which put them on an even playing field.

He sliced his fingers through his hair. "You're right. But you're wrong too. I would never put my team in danger. But I won't put Ruby in danger either. So make the call—am I in or out on this?"

Penn held Gasper's stare for a long heartbeat. He didn't want to be sidelined, and he'd catch hell about it from his other superiors in Operation Freedom Flag who believed in him, but he always followed an order and wouldn't stop doing that now.

After a moment, Penn said, "You're needed here, Jack."

He wasn't prepared for the flood of relief that pumped through his body, leaving him feeling like he'd just gained some ground in his fight.

A fight to keep doing the job he loved...while winning the woman who held his heart.

A deathly silence fell over Ruby's Place, so deep and impenetrable that her restaurant and bar might as well be the first funeral home in White Fog.

Things went on as normal—the girls did their assigned duties. Chores were completed. Ruby taped the menu in the right side to indicate she wasn't taking any shipments today.

But other things were very, very different. Ruby sported a bruise on her cheek that extended to her eye—that shiner Elias had mentioned. The girls whispered about who gave her the bruise and about the dead owner of the bed and breakfast down the street.

She tried to stay busy, but she was just waiting for the other bomb to drop.

Then Big Mike circled the bar and joined her behind the counter. When he grasped her arm hard enough to bruise, she choked down a cry. She wouldn't give the man the satisfaction of seeing he could hurt her, and she raised her head high to glare at him.

"What do you want?"

189

"This." He thrust out his phone.

She really didn't want to see, but her eyes flashed to the device anyway. Her insides filled with dread as she saw her father. Thinner, balder, his eyes two hollows of despair. A trickle of blood ran from his mouth.

Tearing her eyes free, she focused on the big Russian. "What do you want from me?"

"The girls. Jenicka, Polina and Marta."

"I sent Jenicka away for drugs. You know that's my rule, and even your bosses know as much. If they want her, they can go find her."

"Oh, they already know where she is."

"I don't care about her anymore." She hated herself even as she said it. Except she couldn't care about every single person who had ever walked into her life—her soul wasn't big enough to hold them all. She wanted to, but it simply wasn't possible.

Then again, if Jenicka stole into Ruby's Place to ask her for help, she'd do whatever it took in a heartbeat. Without hesitation. Maybe her soul wasn't so iced over after all.

"Marta and Polina ran off with one of their lovers if I have to guess. A couple of the truck drivers who pass through," she told Big Mike.

He narrowed his eyes on her. "We'll see, won't we?"

"I don't lock my girls in. If they choose to leave, I can't stop them."

He raised his hand sharply, and she flinched, preparing for the blow that never came. When she opened her eyes, she found him sneering at her. "Remember who you belong to."

She stared at the man until he circled the bar and returned to his position in front of the restaurant. Then she sagged against the bar, heart pounding with terror she didn't want to feel anymore.

Where could she go? Who could she set free before she took off? The girls — or most of them — and she was pretty sure she could get out of White Fog unnoticed. But that left her father in the lurch.

Maybe it's time to say goodbye to him.

Never. I'll free us both, even if it happens with the last breath I ever take.

A shout came from out front. Her head snapped up, and she ran around the bar before she even gave her body the command. Several of the girls seated in the restaurant doing various tasks jumped to their feet.

"Go upstairs, girls!" she ordered in Russian as she ran to the door. Through the glass, the big, bulky shapes of the special ops team made her blood run cold. But worse was the fight taking place outside.

Elias and Big Mike engaged in a fistfight. To her eyes, it seemed pretty damn fair odds too. Her stomach hit bottom, and she swallowed a cry as Big Mike landed a punch to Elias's stomach that doubled him over.

"Stop!"

Elias looked up at her and straightened, fists raised for the man coming at him even as he tossed a warning for her to get inside.

She couldn't move—her feet were rooted to the concrete. Elias threw a punch, his fist arcing toward Big Mike's face. When it connected in a meaty *thunk,* blood spattered across the sidewalk. She stared down at it, thinking of washing away blood from the woman who'd cut her knee not long ago.

Her head swam. She forced herself to focus on the fight.

"C'mon, Jack!" one of Gasper's teammates called out.

Shouts echoed in her ears. The men were shouting the name Jack. Were they calling Elias by that name?

"You can do better than that, Jack!"

Elias's lips quirked in response.

So he did answer to Jack. There was a lot she didn't know about the man. She certainly didn't know him well enough to give her heart to him.

Yet she'd gone and made that mistake already, hadn't she? She cursed herself and cursed him and damned Big Mike to hell.

Elias dodged a punch. Big Mike ducked to the side to avoid Elias's fist. Why were they playing with each other this way? Either could just pull out a gun and shoot the other, but men would be men and show off.

She swallowed another cry, though she must have made some noise because Elias looked straight at her. His eyes burned. Her stomach flipped at the intensity of his gaze.

From the corner of her eye, she saw a flash. Again, her body moved without thought. She jumped in front of Big Mike.

Chapter Eleven

Ruby crumpled to the sidewalk. And Gasper's heart stopped beating.

With all the strength in him, he shoved Big Mike, sending him flying across the cement. Then Gasper reached for the unconscious woman.

Her face was pale and wan, her eyes closed, but as he scooped her up and took off running with her, her eyelids fluttered.

Where the hell could he even go? The B&B was a crime scene, and the Bratva had eyes on the place. For that matter, they had eyes on Ruby's — it was the only reason he hadn't gone ahead and ended Big Mike's life there and then. Getting in a brawl with a bouncer wouldn't attract as much attention as breaking his neck for laying his hands on Ruby.

As he ran to the SUV still parked along the stark, empty street with her cradled against his chest, he felt an explosion building inside him.

They were fucking around too long on this mission. What happened to completing this mission in a short timeline? They could have lured out the mafia days ago and ended things. But Penn wanted to do every step extra thoroughly in the hope of truly stopping the Russian mafia's foothold in Alaska once and for all.

So while they were biding their time, an innocent man was murdered in his kitchen for harboring one of the Russian girls the mafia considered their property. And they couldn't take out Big Mike the way they had Max. Big Mike was allowed to freely come and go, terrorizing Ruby around every corner.

The chessboard was too big, and Gasper didn't like how many pawns there were on each side. And in the middle stood Ruby, at the biggest risk. He'd just proved that taking his eyes off her for even a second could end in disaster.

He supported her in one arm and whipped open the door of the vehicle. Her head lolled. Carefully, he laid her on the seat, jumped in with her and locked the vehicle. He drew his weapon and placed it within grabbing distance, got behind the wheel and hit the gas.

His first instinct was to get her out of the damn town and away from the people who would hurt her. As he drove, he kept glancing over his shoulder to make sure she was okay. When he found a good place to stop the vehicle, he climbed into the rear with her again.

Perched on the seat next to her, he touched her hand. "Ruby. Can you hear me?"

She was white as bone and too still. His logical mind couldn't think past the emotions roiling inside him. His knowledge of medical emergencies and dozens of traumas he'd witnessed told him that she wasn't going to die. But damn if his heart could catch up. It beat erratically, and his breaths came out in fast gusts.

Leaning over her, he checked her vitals. Pulse rate a little high but steady. Breathing rate coming in target range.

He brushed the thick waves of hair off her face and felt her skull for blood. She'd smacked her head on the pavement when she fell. He hadn't been able to reach her in time.

No sticky, wet blood met his fingertips, and he gently withdrew his hand. "Ruby, wake up. Can you hear me, Ruby?"

She didn't respond. She'd been out for quite a while now, and he didn't like it. In his ear, Penn questioned if everything was all right, and he responded at full volume hoping to jolt her out of it.

She still didn't move.

He cast around for some way to jerk her to consciousness. Suddenly, his mind landed on a name.

"Elliana!"

Her eyelids fluttered. Seeing that the name was dragging her to the surface, and he still had some hold on her, he called her again. "Wake up now, Elliana!"

She moaned softly and her eyes fluttered open.

"Elliana..."

"Stop calling me that."

Her disgruntled tone drew a laugh from him, and relief surged in his veins. He looked into her eyes and saw they were still a bit hazy from her fall, but recognition filled the depths.

He clamped his fingers around hers and lightly squeezed. "How do you feel?"

Her eyes cleared and she attempted to sit up. He held her in place. "Just lie there a second, okay?"

"Where am I?"

"Our SUV."

"What? Why!" She sat up quick and grabbed at her head, which must be spinning.

She looked past him to the window. "*Where* am I?"

"Along the road south of town."

"Are you kidding me? How did I get here?" Angry sparks shot from her gray-blue eyes.

"You don't remember what happened in front of your restaurant?"

She reached for the opposite handle, and before he knew it, she'd jumped out. Dammit, didn't the woman know what was good for her? She took off down the road at a fast clip that belied her state of unconsciousness just a few minutes before.

"Fuck!" He grabbed his gun, stuffed it into his waistband along his spine and took off after her.

"Ruby, stop!"

She didn't turn around. "You took me from my restaurant and drove me all the way out here, miles away! Why?"

"To keep you safe. Big Mike knocked you out and—"

"Because you were showing off your big man skills by trying to beat him up!" She walked faster, hips swaying with each step.

He caught up and grabbed her arm, pulling her to a stop. She wrenched free.

"You don't know what you've done. People like Big Mike realize we've slept together, but now he knows that you care for me too."

He rocked on his heels.

"You're putting a bullseye on my back, Elias! You have to back off."

"I can't! I won't walk away. I care about you."

She barked a laugh. "You don't even know me."

"I damn well do! You're so determined to do what's right by everyone. You care for those girls who are a burden to you. You're loyal to your father and so brave in dealing with the Bratva…"

Though she didn't turn, he knew she was listening.

"I even know that you blow hot and cold with me out of sheer fear, but if things were different, you'd —"

"Shut up. Please stop talking."

How could he? He had to convince her.

"Ruby, I love you."

She whipped around, lips parted, eyes wide.

He spread his hands in a plea.

"No." She shook her head hard. "You're infatuated. Or you want to play hero. Probably both."

"That's not true."

Her hair floated in an arc as she whirled around again. Over her shoulder, she called out, "If you give half a damn about me, you'll leave me alone."

Stunned, he watched her step off the road and into the forest. "Where are you going?"

"Back. I know the way."

"Let me drive you." He raised his voice to be heard as she disappeared in the thick trees.

"Too suspicious!"

Seconds later, he could no longer make out the bright red of her hair.

"Son of a bitch." Fists clenched, he stalked to the SUV and jumped behind the wheel. Breathing hard, he battled a half-dozen emotions he didn't have any idea how to handle.

She was out there in the wilderness between here and White Fog alone.

He could go after her. But he had no doubt she'd run from him. Besides, he had to admit she was right. He'd fucked up by taking her and running. Big Mike and anyone watching the restaurant had seen him.

By now, the Russian mafia knew his team wasn't hanging around for the chili special.

When he took Ruby, they would realize she was tangled up with him. But if she returned alone, it would work in her favor. Any lies she told would be more believable.

Gah—he'd fucked up. He knew it. Could see it with crystal clear clarity now that he had a bit of distance.

Not only had he screwed things up with his team, but he'd thoroughly fucked up with Ruby. For a thrilling heartbeat, when he told her he loved her, he thought she might run to him.

Instead, she'd bolted into the woods.

What was Elias thinking? She couldn't think what to even do with the man. The team was doing their job to shut down the Russian mafia, but that cut off her tie to them—and in turn, her father.

Then the special operative actually told her he loved her! As if she hadn't heard that a few times in her life. She wasn't born yesterday.

As she picked her way through the thick patch of trees that would spit her out close to the main street of White Fog, she mentally argued with him.

You're wrecking all I've worked to create here. You're going to take my business, the safety of my girls...my father's life.

In her mind, he only stared at her, a pleading expression in his eyes.

You don't understand. You only see your side of the situation.

Dammit, not even the imaginary Elias would argue with her. She might as well give up trying.

You don't really love me, she got in the last word.

But her heart jerked in her chest at the memory of his face when he told her. Total joy and love glowed around him like the Northern Lights.

Her body ached from whatever had happened back there on the sidewalk. She only recalled rushing forward to stop Big Mike before he struck Elias, but next thing she knew, she was looking up into Elias's concerned eyes, miles from where she was most needed.

How could she smooth over what he'd done? Big Mike reported everything to the mafia in live time, which meant they already knew she was with Elias.

For all they knew, she'd reneged on her promise to work off her father's debt, and they'd already killed her dad.

Battling back a cry, she hurried faster through the trees. The ground in Alaska always held a bit of moisture, and her feet were soaked, along with the hems of her jeans. Her head pounded, and she was miserable inside and out.

I walked away from a man who told me he loves me...the only man I ever believed means it.

For her own good. For her girls and her father. She had to keep reminding herself what was at stake in loving a man like Elias.

But it was too late for that, wasn't it? That ship had sailed with her heart days ago. She loved him, would run off with him in a blink if not for her responsibilities here.

Tears burned at her eyes, but she wouldn't let them fall. She continued on through the trees and thick underbrush, watchful for bears and anything else she may encounter. She might run a restaurant/bar/brothel and deal with the Russian mafia, but she was a born and bred Alaskan and knew this land.

She was miles from Ruby's Place, and the long walk allowed her time to think up a story. Yes, she'd taken the visitor, Elias, to bed and that made him believe he had some hold over her. So after she stepped into a fight between him and Big Mike, he thought he could just take off with her.

She'd set him straight by running from him and making her way back where she belonged, under the Bratva's thumb.

She'd leave off that last bit, but it sounded credible to her own way of thinking. With luck, they would buy it. She could always put on her dumb redhead act with Big Mike and whoever else tried to pressure her into confessing something more was going on. Wouldn't be the first time.

As the forest lightened, she saw the trees were thinning. She leaped over a log and ran the rest of the way to the forest's edge. She popped out into a small clearing she knew to be between the truck stop and town.

Her wet socks chafed in her boots, and she felt a blister rising on her heel. Pushing on as fast as she could, she kept the roof of Ruby's Place in sight. She had a stitch in her side and her mouth was dry, though the constant pangs in her heart were what really weighed her steps.

She was walking away from the man she wanted. And that hurt.

Nobody stood out on the sidewalk. She angled to the rear of the building and slipped inside. She hadn't even taken a step before big hands clasped around her upper arms. She cried out as her feet were separated from the floor and then her backside met with a hard chair.

"Would people stop picking me up without my permission?" she blasted the man standing before her.

A stranger and yet not entirely unrecognizable to her. She'd seen him walking in and out of the room where her father was kept.

203

"Where were you?" he asked in a harsh Russian accent.

She raised her jaw and met his stare despite her quivering stomach. "That idiot must have taken me away. I woke up in the middle of nowhere. That man must have used me as a human shield to get out."

He didn't shift his attention from her. He was waiting for her to give some sign that what she said was a lie. Yet she was used to lying—her poor grandmother would roll over in her grave to hear it—and she held her ground.

The silence stretched between them. Each second felt as though it ticked down her life—or her father's. If the man who tormented her dad was here in this kitchen with her, what did that mean? Was her father even alive?

The big man made a sudden move, and she flinched, bracing for a blow. But he simply folded his arms and gave her a nod. "You don't leave again. Understand?"

She nodded. Her stomach still fluttered, and she felt hot and cold, but relief settled in her veins. He bought her story.

One of her girls walked into the kitchen, holding a tray stacked with dirty dishes. She looked between Ruby and the dude and then started to back out.

But Ruby saw her as a savior. "Wait! Come in and put down your dishes." She waved her in.

Thankfully, the man left them alone. Ruby watched him walk out. Breathing heavily, she dropped her face into her hands.

"Are you all right?" The girl touched her arm.

Needing a friend now, she lifted her face and then pulled the girl into her arms. She immediately hugged her back. That human touch reminded her of why she was here, doing what she did.

The girl patted Ruby's back. The comfort didn't ease her pain at rejecting Elias, but it would have to do for now, wouldn't it?

After they parted, Ruby offered her a smile. "Thank you for that."

She gave a nod.

"I'm going to take a hot bath." Until she spoke the words, she didn't realize what a good idea it was. She was wet, chilled and devastated. Fear didn't even register on her radar at this point. At least she could breathe easier knowing that the thug sent here to keep an eye on her believed her tale.

In the bathroom, she sat on the edge of the tub to adjust the water to a perfect steamy hot temperature. She reached into a jar and dropped a few flower petals in to scent the water, a luxury her grandmother always spoiled her with as a child.

Then she stripped off her damp clothes and sank into the fragrant depths. The heat relaxed her muscles, which in turn slowed her spinning mind.

She kept returning to Elias, though. How must he feel? After confessing his love, she practically ran into the woods to get away from him. He didn't even know if she'd made it back to Ruby's Place. Though he could easily ask one of the girls.

That line of thought led to her need to get the girls out of here—fast. Before they were sold into even more terrible lives.

She sat up straighter in the tub. When had she decided such a thing? With a jolt, she realized she was no longer just swimming along, pushed by the current of her life. She was swimming against it. She wanted to fight.

Elias put that fight into her. He made her see a future—at long last. He made her see her own worth, and in turn she wanted to fight for the worth of every girl under her care.

She was an informant for the United States. A pawn for the Russians. A daughter and a granddaughter.

She was Elias's lover.

His love.

Pulling strength from all those things, it hit her. If she set her mind to it, what couldn't she do?

She could be unstoppable.

Gasper's fingers twitched into fists, and he shook them out. Again. But seconds later, they were back to forming fists.

He stared at the darkened windows of Ruby's Place while the fog was rolling in. When Penn gave the order for Winston and Lipton to patrol the restaurant and bar, Gasper had forced his way into the group — and was shocked when Penn didn't even argue with him.

A team of state troopers watched over the bed and breakfast, and that freed up the rest of the Xtreme Ops to keep eyes on the water. They had reason to believe a shipment might be coming in tonight.

"You plan on going inside?" Lipton's question drifted to him through the thick fog.

"She doesn't want me to." He'd all but admitted to his love affair with Ruby to his captain's second-in-command. At this point, he was done caring who knew. She was still in danger, and he couldn't see anything past that. He would guard her life with his own — no way in hell would the mafia get their hands on her.

"Falling out?" Lipton asked.

"A difference of opinion." He unclenched his fists again, letting the blood rush into his hands.

"She decided she doesn't like your ugly ass," Lipton joked.

Gasper stared at her blackened window. Any humor he might have responded with felt miles from him now. He couldn't crack a joke if he tried.

He pushed out a sigh. "She thinks we're fucking up her situation."

"We are. But things usually have to get worse before all hell breaks loose and we get the people free. You know that."

Hell, he did, all too well. He pinched the bridge of his nose. "I wasn't thinking about that when I ran with her."

"I know."

Pivoting, he pierced Lipton with a stare. "I know you do. You'd do anything for Jenna."

"Damn straight I would. I would have laid down my life to save her in that forest when the bomber was on the loose."

"I feel the same. But how the hell do we get her and all the girls out safe *and* stop these guys? Is it me, or do our superiors want us to lose this battle?"

Lipton's eyes glittered in the faint cast of moonlight. The world looked creepy as hell, with a thin glow of light coming from the moon and the fog shifting around them like ghosts dancing. In the distance, he heard the crash of waves on the rocky shore and even the faint rustle of fishermen unloading their hauls.

"Do you actually believe we'll ever drive the Russian mafia out of Alaska? Organized crime's been in the US practically since the country was founded. We're never gonna fully get them out," Lipton told him.

"No, of course not. You're right. I realize as much — it's just hard to swallow. Working to beat down an enemy, but knowing they'll just pop up again, stronger and with more backup."

Lipton stared at him for a long minute. "We'll free the woman and her father."

Something in Lipton's voice made him lift his head. "What news of her father? Any progress in finding him?"

"They followed a money trail from a year ago, and it leads to some buildings owned by the original smuggler he gambled with. They think the father's being kept in one of those properties."

"In Anchorage?"

"Most of the properties are located in the city, yeah. Rentals and such. They also checked out the smuggler's associates. Take a look at this." He held out his phone, and Gasper walked over with stealthily quiet steps to see.

"Recognize these assholes?" Lipton asked.

A photo of Mikhail and another of Maxim filled the screen. Lipton swiped his thumb, and Russian prison mugshots came into view. They knew the bouncers had done time, but now that they saw their list of crimes, all those tattoos gained in prison made sense.

Gasper scanned his surroundings for danger, but he directed his question at his teammate. "So, what's the plan?"

Lipton often knew what Penn had in mind, but he focused on the perimeter rather than Gasper.

"Lip." His tone was harsh.

"I don't know anything for certain."

"But you and Penn did discuss the plan."

"Nothing's finalized, and I can't say more than that."

"I assume we're sending someone in after the father. The shipment's due in here very soon, and the girls will be sent out." Gasper's gaze was dragged again and again to Ruby's bedroom window. Was she tossing and turning? Or asleep like an angel?

He swallowed hard. "If we really are planning to divide and conquer...it must happen at the same time, or someone will get killed."

Chapter Twelve

Ruby searched the countertop for the new menus to tape onto the front door. She shifted around a few trays and a stack of clean dishes that still needed put on the shelf.

"Anushka."

The girl looked up from the giant pot of chili she was manning. Just the smell of chili made Ruby think of Elias stripping down to his undies.

"Did you see the menus anywhere?" Ruby asked. She wanted to ask where that guy sent to babysit her was but refrained. She hadn't seen him in a while, and she suspected one of her girls might be entertaining him upstairs.

"Big Mike talked to that other guy and he already took them."

Ruby's heart pattered to a dull stop. "Took them?"

"Yes, he already taped them in the window."

She ran to see for herself. When her gaze locked on the front and she saw the menus taped in the left side, terror struck.

Shipments only happened on Tuesdays and Sundays. This wasn't Tuesday or Sunday. What was happening?

"Big Mike?" Where was the man? Not in his usual post by the entrance. She rushed to peer out, but he wasn't on the sidewalk out front either.

"Where is he?" she whispered under her breath. Chills broke over her.

They'd cut her out of the loop, which meant they didn't trust her.

Quickly, she took the stairs two at a time to reach the top. She did a sweep of the girls' rooms and found every woman accounted for. Ice sat like a giant block in her chest, even after seeing the girls hadn't been stolen or sold out from under her nose.

She had to fix the rift in her relationship with the Bratva. But how? They'd know if she was kissing up.

What could she do? Who could she count on?

The realization hit her as if a spotlight lit up a billboard. The answer had been there the whole time.

Elias.

They had promised to keep her safe, and well, she felt far from it this very minute. Realizing that Big Mike was communicating with the mafia behind her back, and was now completing tasks she'd been told to do…

She rushed through the restaurant and strode into her office.

From the kitchen, Anushka called, "Did you find him?"

But Ruby slammed her office door and settled at her laptop. All her communications were watched by the men holding her father, but Elias had given her a way to bypass the mafia and to reach him if the need every arose.

Did she need him? More than he knew. More than she had admitted to.

With shaking hands, she typed in the link, and it took her directly to an email box. In a few quick sentences, she relayed the details about the shipment coming early and how they'd gone over her head directly to Big Mike.

After she said what she needed to say, she let her fingers hover over the keys, thinking about what she *wanted* to say.

At that moment, the door opened. She felt the overgrown man taking up the entrance, his stare unnerving as hell. Pretending to be engrossed in her work, she didn't look away from the email she'd typed to Elias but hadn't sent yet.

"What do you need, Big Mike? I'm working on the books, and you know I can't be disturbed. If I get a single number wrong—"

He cut her off, "Anushka said you were looking for me."

She met his stare. "I can't even remember what I needed now." She pretended to think, tapping a fingertip against her lips. Hardly any air moved through her lungs, and under the desk, her knees were practically knocking together.

If he came over here, how would she hide the email to Elias?

"Oh! I remember Could you move that big carton of whiskey to the bar so I can put it away? It's too heavy for me to move." She offered him a smile. "Thanks. Close the door on your way out."

The latter was just the right amount of bitchiness of the normal Ruby, and Big Mike nodded before backing out of the room.

Her fingers flew over the keys.

I'm sorry about everything. Please don't leave me alone in this. We can't let these guys win.

She hesitated before adding, "Love, Ruby."

Before she could change her words, she hit send. Then she sat there, heart pounding and her breaths rushing out too fast as she imagined the message moving through the air, sailing straight to Elias. Too late, she thought he might not be the person to receive the message. Did it matter, though? He'd hear about it and come to help her.

To make it look as if she really was working hard, she sat in her office for half an hour. No email came back to her. Nobody texted or called, but that wasn't surprising. The team knew she was being watched, and they wouldn't put her at risk.

How stupid she'd been to drive Elias away. What if something happened to him, and he left the world believing she didn't give a damn? She of all people knew life was short. She'd gotten mere seconds to say goodbye to her father as they dragged him out of the bar and shoved him into a van. She only saw him on a screen after he'd been beaten. She never got a chance to tell him she loved him and would do anything in her power to save him.

Emotions bubbled inside her. They churned like the sea. She loved Elias. Damn the man. Why did he have to show up now when she was in the middle of a personal hell?

Her grandmother had all the superstition of a sailor, and if she were here, she'd tell Ruby that everything happens for a reason and when it's meant to happen. Which meant Elias came to break her free of the Bratva's hold ...and possibly to break her free of herself.

The few stolen moments with him—in the laundry room up or in her bed—were the happiest she could remember in her life. He made her feel...alive. And for a woman who'd been slogging through the motions of a bad situation, that was huge.

She went to the kitchen and spent some time talking to Anushka just to make her think everything was business as usual. They discussed cornbread and

Ruby suggested making an extra batch since chili was a popular special and they always ran out.

As Anushka whirled around the kitchen to gather more ingredients, Ruby breathed a sigh of relief.

She went through the motions of helping her mix up the cornbread batter and poured it into several greased baking pans. When she had all the pans lined up in the oven, she wiped her hands on a dishtowel and walked out into the restaurant.

Big Mike's back was to her, but she saw by the way he stood that he was on the phone with somebody. She froze, head cocked, listening hard to his low rumbling words. The conversation didn't make much sense on this end, until he said, "Pull up the shipment."

Her mouth dried out. Pull up the shipment from the depths of the sea? The waterproof bag filled with drugs that the runners attached to the buoy—that same buoy she'd sent the special ops team to inspect. And from what she knew, they'd taken one of the bags.

As soon as the mafia tried to fish that bag out of the water, they'd find it was missing. And then what?

She tried to tell herself that she wasn't involved in that job. For that matter, she hadn't known Big Mike was either. But clearly, he and probably Max too, were more involved in this game than she'd ever thought. They weren't only watching over her to ensure she did what she was told to. They were calling the shots.

Oh God. How long had this been going on? She had to get another message to Elias. She didn't care if he beat the man to a pulp—he had to stop him from exerting more power and giving the order to kill her father.

She slowly backed out of the room and pushed through the kitchen door. Anushka was humming a tune and thankfully didn't look up at Ruby as she hurried to her office.

She only dropped into the chair behind her desk for just seconds before she was on her feet again, pacing.

If the team was out at that buoy and the Russians came in to collect their goods...

Her stomach balled up like someone had driven a fist into it. She settled her hand over the spot, breathing through the pain she only felt internally. If they killed Elias, she couldn't forgive herself.

She had to try to warn the team.

Casting a desperate look around her office for some reason to go out, her stare landed on a pile of mail already bearing stamps. A walk to the corner mailbox would be just the excuse.

She snatched up the mail and grabbed her light jacket from the arm of the chair. The mornings were cool enough to always require a coat, and the wind was coming off the sea today. When she headed for the back, Big Mike's voice stopped her.

"Where do you think you're going?"

217

"To mail these bills before the electric company cuts our power." She arched a brow at him, tempting him to stop her from running the business fronting his disgusting human trafficking and drug trade.

"I'll take them." He started toward her.

At that moment, Anushka looked up and met Ruby's stare. Whatever she saw on her face had the woman moving fast — too fast.

"I'll be right back!" Ruby called just as Anushka hit the handle of the big chili pot. In slow motion it tipped off the range. Ruby didn't stick around to see the mess that followed, but she heard Big Mike's bellow as hot chili splashed over him.

She tucked the mail inside her coat and took off running. White Fog was the size of a crumb, so it shouldn't be too difficult to locate the men. She headed straight for the dock. When she came to a stop, breathing hard, a low whistle sounded. She jerked in a circle, looking for the source.

One of the special ops team stepped out from between two shipping crates sitting on the dock. She'd never heard his name, only that he ordered iced tea and the occasional beer he never drank.

"You're looking for Jack."

She blinked at him.

"Gasper."

"Yes." She hadn't caught her breath yet, and she was well aware that Big Mike would be looking for her the minute he changed out of his chili-covered clothes. Thank God for Anushka. When she got to the restaurant, she'd give her a big hug and the rest of the day off.

"He's not here, but you can give me any message you have for him." The man was so big and imposing she might be scared of him if she didn't know what his job was here.

"When will he be back?"

He looked to the water. She followed his stare but didn't see a single craft on the waves. "Sorry, I can't say."

"Can't or won't?" Anger rose inside her.

He looked into her eyes. "Can't. I'm not sure when he'll return."

"Where did he go?"

He gave her a flat look she read to mean he wouldn't say.

She huffed out a breath. "Fine. Tell him that… Oh, screw it! If he isn't even here, he can't do anything anyhow. There's a shipment coming in early."

"We know."

"You…" She gulped and bit off the words she wanted to blast him with. "I guess I just risked my life to come here and warn you. Good luck stopping it!" She whirled and stalked off.

"Ruby," he called.

She stopped to look at him again.

"I'm coming with you."

"No you're not." She took a step backward.

"If your life's in jeopardy—"

"It's been in jeopardy since my father lost that hand of poker. I've survived this long—I'll be fine." With that, she hurried from the dock, keeping an eye out for Big Mike or any of the Bratva ready to take her down.

She was no idiot, though—that guy from the dock was definitely tailing her. She ignored him and dumped the mail into the box before returning to Ruby's Place. When she walked in, Anushka was singing to herself as she scrubbed the spilled chili off the walls and floor.

She looked up at Ruby with a smile.

Thank you, Ruby mouthed to her, and then she grabbed a cloth to help her.

Gasper had a bad feeling about leaving White Fog. He also had a bad feeling about going to Anchorage. And yet what choice did he have but to take his captain's order and join the mission to rescue Ruby's father?

Why wasn't he on that ship with the Coast Guard, headed out to intercept the smugglers at the buoy? He couldn't help but think Penn sent him on purpose, and that rankled. He had to prove his worth on this quest to locate Ruby's father and see him safe.

Shit was about to go down at Ruby's Place, and he burned to be there to protect her. He would just have to leave it to his team to do it for him. He had to trust them to keep his woman safe.

Not my woman. She didn't want anything to do with him, and he understood even if it hurt.

He listened to Lipton and Winston going over the particulars of freeing Ruby's father. Their sources told them there were no guards during the day, when the man was locked into his prison. He kept half an ear on their discussion, but he knew everything they recounted, so he let his mind drift to the rest of the team.

Half on a boat with the Coast Guard already out on the water. And two Xtreme Ops teammates were at the bar to keep the girls safe and get the bouncer out of the way.

Where was Ruby in all this? He envisioned that chessboard again. Had they done anything to push the odds in her favor? He didn't know anymore.

"Jack?"

He looked up at Lipton.

They were holed up a few blocks from where they believed the father to be hidden, biding their time and waiting for word from the Anchorage PD who were staking out the house that the coast was clear.

"What's up?" he asked Lipton.

"I don't know if I should tell you this or not."

He went cold inside. "You already started, so you better finish." He didn't mean to clamp his hands into fists—his body took over.

"Broshears just gave word that Ruby came to the dock looking for you."

Christ. His heart felt stabbed with pain and fear and longing.

"Is she okay?"

"He followed her to Ruby's Place to make sure, so yeah."

He owed Broshears a drink when they got to base.

"What did she need?" Dragging information from Lipton lately was like extracting a pebble encased in cement.

"She came to warn us that the shipment's coming early."

"Fuck." They'd found out hours before the ship was spotted on the water headed to the buoy. And if she knew, that meant she was in danger. But when was Ruby not in danger?

He didn't care if she hated him, or that their relationship could never work out. He still wanted to be there to watch over her.

Struggling to deal with his feelings, he walked to the window of the apartment where they were set up and looked out on the ugly, overgrown patch of grass across the way.

"Jack?" Lipton's voice shook him.

"Now I know why Penn sent me away."

"What do you mean?" Winston leaned against the wall, arms folded in a nonchalant pose.

"You guys call me the jack-of-all-trades, but I can't master this one thing."

"What thing?" Lipton asked.

He scrubbed a hand over his face. He was tired. He wanted to find Ruby, lock her against his body and fall into a healing sleep with her.

"I can't separate my personal life from my duty." His voice came out with an edge of the anger he directed at himself. "I've never had an issue before."

"You've never been in love before."

He looked to Lipton. He was close to all the guys, but typically he confided in Shadow. Having this new bond with Lipton left him even more grateful to have these men in his life.

"Man, listen to us." His lips quirked. "We sound like a soap opera. I'm in love with the owner of a bar, she rejected me, and still I'm going crazy with the need to make sure she's safe."

Lipton chuckled. "Guess that means I'd better confide my own little secret."

Winston and Gasper stared at Lipton, waiting.

"Jenna's pregnant. With twins."

For some reason this struck them all as hilarious, and laughing through blinding tears, Gasper walked over to clap Lipton on the shoulder.

"Congrats, man. I guess you'd better ask for a raise in pay to support your family."

They laughed harder. Gasper and Lipton focused on Winston. "What's your story, bro? Your mom's got amnesia and now she thinks she's your sister?" Gasper swiped new tears of mirth out of his eyes. They razzed Winston for a while until they calmed down.

"All kidding aside, Jack, you're holding up pretty damn well. If Jenna were in danger, I'd be losing my shit." Lipton took out his pocket knife and started cleaning his nails.

"That doesn't make me feel better, man."

Lipton sobered. "She's in good hands. The guys at the bar won't let her get hurt. They've been posted there to protect all the women. Beckett and Day are damn good, and Pax's replacement is one hell of a shot. I'm hopin' Penn keeps him on the team after Paxton returns."

"If he returns." Winston's quiet statement rang with too much truth.

"We gotta keep our heads in the game. Be ready to hit that rental property and free the old man as soon as we get word," Lipton said.

"Copy that." Gasper looked out the window again. Through the heavy cloud cover hanging over Anchorage, a ray of sun broke through. He was far from superstitious, but maybe loving Ruby made him tap into his gut feelings more than usual. Because now, he saw that beam of sunlight slanting through the sky and knew without a doubt they'd be successful today. They'd see her father safe.

Then it would be time to fight for a place in Ruby's heart.

His phone buzzed, and next thing he knew a message flashed on his screen. An email from Ruby, saying the shipment was coming early and that they had to win against these guys.

She signed it with "Love, Ruby." His heart ached. What did that mean for them?

He barely processed the thought before they got the call. Gasper burst outside first.

He knew the drill—bust down the door of the house and find the old man. Shoot anything that moved besides the old man. Get him out, seek medical attention if necessary—though from the images he'd seen on Max's phone, Ruby's father would definitely require medical treatment.

They had to hide him too. It was far too easy for the Russians to put their hands on him again, and this time they wouldn't be kind enough to keep him alive. Or maybe the true kindness would have been death rather than torture.

They ran the few blocks to the house. The entire street of homes was rundown, needing updates the owners couldn't afford. Broken sidewalks and falling-down porches and enough moss growing in places moss shouldn't even be growing were only a few indications that the inside of the house wouldn't be better.

Lipton gave the signal, and Gasper aimed his weapon at the lock. He shot it open, and the door swung inward as if a spectral hand opened it to invite them in.

The adrenaline rush was something Gasper lived for. It'd been too long since he actually did more than bide his time and wait for the perfect moment. This was their moment.

Rushing into the house, he and Winston took turns clearing rooms. The kitchen reeked and rats scurried into hiding spots. The sticky floors underfoot made him want to look down but at the same time he avoided doing so. He didn't want to see what was underfoot as they blasted through the house searching for Ruby's father.

Winston reached the room first. "Jack."

He strode toward the door with several locks and a chain to hold it shut.

"Somebody really didn't want him getting free."

Shooting the lock off meant the bullet could possibly strike the old man within. "I'll have to pick them."

"Hurry," Lipton said from his six. "We don't know how much time we've got. I checked the place for a security system, and I don't see one, which is a direct indication there is someone watching this place."

"Maybe not. A harmless old man who can't escape his room is only important to his daughter." Jack stuck the tool into the first lock and popped it. Seconds later, he opened another. "Give me something to cut through this chain." He focused on the inner workings of the lock, found the next sweet spot and tripped that lock too.

Winston had bolt cutters in hand, pulled out of thin air, and he crunched through the heavy steel link.

"On my lead. Three, two…" Gasper shoved open the door and set eyes on the man shriveled into a ball on a dirty cot. The man reared up, crying out for them not to hurt him. In his battered face, he saw some of the features he shared with Ruby.

Gasper's heart lifted with victory. They'd found him.

He crossed the room to the old man and looked down at him. "Mr. Rynizski, we're getting you out of here. And I want you to know your daughter is safe."

At least she was an hour ago. He only prayed that was still the case.

Chapter Thirteen

"Get him out of here!" Lipton's bellow came between blasts of gunfire.

Gasper took one look at the man on the bed and knew he was too weak to walk, much less sprint through bullets. With no other choice, he hooked the man beneath the arms and lifted him. He weighed little, and Gasper carried heavier in his pack on a boring Tuesday.

He tossed him over his shoulder, locked an arm around his thighs and ran.

Archer Rynizski smelled like sweat and stale breath and something worse underneath those odors. He'd taken enough beatings and seen enough torture that Gasper wouldn't be shocked if he had an infection, maybe in those ruined fingers he'd seen on screen.

In a few strides, he faced the empty hall leading to the staircase he needed to navigate while being shot at. The mafia showed up seconds after they burst into the house, and they had Lipton and Winston pinned down in these rooms. Fuck if Gasper could help his brothers right now, though.

He stepped out of the room and spotted Lipton jerking his head in as a bullet sliced past him and slammed into the doorframe. Fuck, they were all going it alone.

With his weapon up, he provided his own covering fire, making sure his bullets didn't hit either of his men. Over his shoulder, Archer hung limply. Had he passed out from terror?

Didn't matter now. A scream sounded from his side as he booked it to the exit. Chances that the mafia didn't have the house surrounded seemed slim, but again, he had few options. See Archer to safety and complete his mission, or stick around and fight.

A man jumped into view. Gasper didn't think— he saw the weapon in the man's hand, and he took the shot.

The thug flew backward, and Gasper kept running. Thank God the Anchorage PD was on site and provided enough cover for him to make it to the street. A paramedic unit also sat waiting at the corner. The stretch of road seemed endless, when really it took mere seconds to move Ruby's father to the waiting medics.

He dumped him on the ground and whirled to race to his brothers. He was having a déjà vu moment of running Paxton to safety.

Two more police units rolled up. An officer jumped out at the sight of him toting a weapon, but then he realized he was one of the good guys.

He'd never tuned out of the communication between Lipton and Winston, but their words were sharper in his hearing now.

"Two on my nine."

"In my sights. Duck, Lip."

Gunfire sounded. Then silence.

From Gasper's experience, silence was never good.

With stealthy steps, he cleared the back door and entered the house. He was good at picking out hiding spots and shot two men before they knew what hit them.

"Down two," he told his team.

"Do we have a body count?" Lipton asked.

"Six," came Winston's response.

A big police officer stepped in behind him. "We spotted a suspicious vehicle parked down the block."

Gasper looked at him. "Empty?"

He nodded.

"Run the plates."

"One step ahead of ya." He grinned. "Do what you gotta do here. I got your six."

"'Preciate it."

Together they moved through the rooms, sweeping every corner for more men hiding. The creak of floorboards upstairs along with the whispered communications in his ear between Winston and Lipton told him the guys were doing the same.

"Clear."

Seconds later, the guys' boots sounded on the stairs. Gasper and the officer completed their search of the lower level of the house. The officer called for drug enforcement to come take a look at the kitchen, where baggies of drugs were scattered on the counter along with a scale and other paraphernalia.

"Looks like they were doing more than torturing a man here," he said.

Gasper nodded. "Do what you need to do. We got what we came here for." He reached out and bumped knuckles with the officer.

Outside, more officers milled around the property, stretching police tape and snapping photos. He and his team headed straight for the ambulance on the corner. They were just loading Ruby's father into the back.

Gasper put out a hand to stop them. "I want to ride with him if possible."

"Sure. Get in."

Lipton gave him a lift of his jaw in recognition. "We'll meet you at the hospital, Jack."

He gripped the doorframe and launched himself into the rear of the ambulance. Settling along the side, he examined Ruby's father. His red hair was thin and

231

matted. Blood stained his shirt and crusted on a scab over his brow that looked to be a source of infection.

He was starved and sickly, but he was alive.

Reaching out, Gasper rested a hand over the man's bony one. He opened his eyes. Confusion and fear lit the depths, a flint gray similar to Ruby's.

"You're safe now," he told him.

He closed his eyes and then slowly opened them. "I owe you my thanks." His voice was reedy.

"I did it for Ruby."

"You know my daughter?"

"Yes. She's very special."

A tear trickled from the corner of his eye. "She is."

"You put her in danger."

His throat worked for a moment. Gasper could go easy on the man—maybe he should. But fact was, if Archer hadn't gotten in over his head with the Bratva, he and Ruby wouldn't be in this situation.

"You're right. Did they hurt her? Is she okay?"

Gasper thought of Ruby's bruised face and God knew what else she'd endured before he knew her.

"She's strong. She's survived," he told the old man.

"Thank God for that."

"She's headstrong too. She refused to leave when she should have long ago."

The medic who was fussing with the man's IV glanced up at Gasper as if to tell him not to upset the old man. But he deserved to be punished for putting his daughter in danger. Putting himself above his love for her was his first mistake, and luckily Ruby's strength had pulled her through. But Gasper wasn't letting him off the hook for hurting someone he was supposed to love—and who Gasper loved.

"You care about her." Archer's voice broke.

"Yes."

"Does she care about you?"

How to answer that? When he thought of Ruby's eyes when he claimed her body, he believed she felt more than lust. And she'd signed the email with "Love, Ruby."

But she'd pushed him away too.

It might be her nature to reject anything good for herself.

None of that mattered—he would be there for her until the day he died and never ask a thing of her in return. He might not have any skills in relationships, but he'd learned how to love.

He met the old man's eyes. "I don't know the answer to your question. But if she agrees, I'll take her out of White Fog and let her have a fresh start."

He closed his eyes again and didn't speak for a long time. When he did, Gasper had to lean in to catch the faint words.

"She should go with you. She deserves better —
always did."

Ruby's hands shook. She didn't think she could hide
her emotions any longer — she was too scared.

Big Mike hadn't taken his eyes off her since he
returned from God knew where. The only mercy was
the fact she didn't have Max to deal with too.

But people had been coming and going all day
long. Sooner or later, someone would tell her to sneak
the girls out the back and load them into a truck.
What then? She wouldn't let them go — not this time.
She'd failed too many girls over the course of a year.
If Elias had taught her anything, it was that she
needed to fight for what she believed in. To give her
life for the cause if it came down to it.

She moved through the restaurant, watching
every patron closely. Truck drivers and fishermen
might be her contact, which could be any number of
people all spooning her chili special into their
mouths.

The only person she'd ruled out as being her
contact was the older woman dressed in khaki slacks,
a light sweater with an anchor on it and the white
sneakers Ruby'd come to associate with tourists in
White Fog.

Setting a couple of plates in front of two customers, she offered what smile she could and told them to enjoy their lunches.

When the door opened, all the hair rose on her body. She felt a stare on her spine and hardly wanted to turn around and see who was standing there.

Slowly, she pivoted enough to cast a look from the corner of her eye.

Her heart flipped over and thudded flat on its back. Two of the guys from the special ops team stood in her restaurant, looking for an empty table.

Why, today of all days, was it her chili special? She needed the restaurant to be empty.

One of the men gave her a nod as he casually walked to a table and pulled out a chair. His buddy followed. She had to wait on them, didn't she?

Grounding herself, she made her way toward them. "Wh-what can I bring you two?"

The dark-haired man who'd been on the dock pulled something out of his pocket, set it on the table and covered it with his hand. Holding her stare, he pushed it toward her. "I'll have a lemonade for now."

She threw a look around for Big Mike. The last thing she needed was for him to see her accepting a note from this man. Thinking on her feet, she set her tray down as if it was too heavy, and when she picked it up again, she clasped the note in her palm.

"Make that two lemonades," the other guy said.

"Be right back." On legs that felt wooden, she walked into the kitchen and set down the tray. Anushka looked up from ladling chili into bowls. Ruby tossed her a nod and rushed into the bathroom to be alone.

As soon as she slammed the door and twisted the lock, she unfolded the tiny square of paper.

Gasper is rescuing your father. Will be there soon. If the mission's a success, I'll order two bowls of chili.

Her lips parted on a silent cry. It was happening—the team was going to break her father free. But what would happen to her once the Russians found out their captive had gone missing? They'd come straight here.

Fear only rose inside her for a split second before joy flooded in to replace it. Her father would be safe, after all this time! And by Gasper's hands. Surely the man deserved a steak and a blow job as a reward for such a thing.

She wanted to laugh, but tears trickled out of her eyes instead. A mess of emotions, she blinked through the droplets enough to read the note one more time. Then she tore it up and flushed it down the toilet.

Standing there for a long minute, she dragged in deep breaths to collect herself. She splashed her face with water and dried her eyes. When she walked into the kitchen, Big Mike stood there waiting for her.

She cocked a brow at him in challenge. "Can't a woman take a piss?"

"You should be more ladylike, Ruby."

"Fuck you," she sang out as she passed him to push through the kitchen door. She threw a look at the guys still seated at the table and at the packed restaurant. When her stare lit on a man sitting alone at a table, her chest threatened to cave in.

She'd seen enough men come to take the girls away to recognize him for what he was. Abby started toward him, and Ruby blocked her way. "I'll take that table. You bring the guys two lemonades, okay?"

Abby gave her a strange look but nodded.

With a thundering heart, Ruby crossed the room to the man. She'd never seen him before, but then again, the Bratva sent a new man every time. Whether or not the men they commissioned to make a pickup at Ruby's Place knew what cargo they hauled was a mystery to her. She didn't care either. Over her dead body would he take her girls.

"Hello," she said coolly.

He looked up from the menu. "I'm here for the catch of the day."

Oh.

Hell.

She wanted to run. Scream. Bash him over the head with a tray or stab him in the eye with her pen.

237

Anything to get him out of here.

Of course he was here to collect the girls. The catch of the day was code the same way the bowls of chili were to the special operatives eyeing her up from across the room.

She caught the dark-haired one's stare and held it for a moment longer than was custom.

"Anything to drink this afternoon?" she asked the man she swung her attention to.

He leaned back in his chair, giving her a clear view of a weapon tucked into the waist of his pants.

Unsure if she should be relieved he was here or more frightened, she tried for a smile that probably looked as if she was about to throw up. "How about a drink while you wait?" she pressured.

He issued a sigh. "Fine. Iced tea."

She didn't feel a bit happy about the fact she'd talked him into waiting. His job was to load up as fast as possible and move the girls to the next destination, wherever that was.

Big Mike intercepted her before she poured the man's iced tea. "What are you doing?"

"Fetching him a drink."

He leveled a glare at her. "You know what he's here for."

"Yes." She waved at the packed restaurant. "Do you think it's wise to sneak the girls down the stairs in plain sight now? We need some of these customers to leave first. You should have thought about this before you decided to make it a shipment day."

He looked around. "Fine. But you'd better not be trying to pull something on me."

"You know I have a lot at stake — why would I do that?" *Please, Elias, get my father out fast!*

She almost knocked over the iced tea she'd just poured and shooed Big Mike away. "Let me do my job!"

He left her alone, but he positioned himself at the door where he could see every move she made. After she set the tea before the man, she caught a twitch from the special operative who'd passed her the note.

Her stomach flipped over this time, instead of her heart. With measured steps, she reached his table.

His eyes drilled into her for what felt like minutes even though she knew nothing more than seconds passed.

Dropping his attention to the menu in his hands, he said, "Is that your contact person?" as casually as he would order a burger.

She gave him a pleasant smile and nod in return.

"He's watching you like a hawk."

"That makes me feel loads better," she said.

He closed his menu and looked up into her eyes. "Maybe this will — we'll have two bowls of chili."

Ruby made it as far as the kitchen before she burst into tears. She couldn't even hold in the noisy tears and let it all out.

Her father…safe at last. And she had Elias to thank.

The sound of the door swinging open behind her made her glance over her shoulder. She went cold and dead inside.

"What are you crying for?" Big Mike demanded.

God, what she wouldn't give for another pot of scalding chili. She'd hit him with it and make sure to drench his balls this time.

Her insides coiled. "Can't a woman cry in her own kitchen?"

"Something is up. If you don't tell me what it is right this minute…"

Her fury rose, smoke and oil that darkened and smothered everything in her being with the need to hurt this man. She took a step backward, within reach of the knife block. All she needed was one stab. One. Good. Jab.

He narrowed his eyes on her, his stare icy. "Don't test me! All it takes is a call to end your father's life."

She met his glare with a dark look of her own. Now she knew he was bluffing or he was clueless about her father's welfare and whereabouts.

When she took a step toward him, shock registered on his face.

She opened her mouth to describe the length and girth of cactus he should shove up his ass when a crash sounded in the restaurant. She pushed by Big Mike and ran into the front. A single glance showed her that the room had been cleared of customers and the guy sent by the mafia was on his feet.

So were the two special operatives.

If she had to put money on anybody, it would be the muscled men who fought for their country. But the mafia man would play dirty and who said it would be a fair fight?

Ruby stumbled into the room, propelled by a massive hand in the center of her back. She nearly pitched forward and grabbed for the nearest table. Sticky soda had been spilled at some point — the crash she'd heard, probably — and splashed under her boots.

"I told you to clear out with the others," the mafia's guy ground out, his focus on the special operatives.

The dark-haired man reached a lazy hand across the table and snatched up his glass. "Haven't finished my drink." His eyes found hers, a silent question in them.

Are you okay?

She gave him the barest hint of a nod in return. What she wouldn't do to have Elias here right now. She trusted his men to keep her safe, but it wasn't the same as having Elias's warm arms around her.

Big Mike latched on to her forearm, and she cried out. The special operative started forward, and his buddy stopped him. Big Mike's mouth at her ear lifted bile in her throat.

"Go upstairs and find the girls."

"I—" She cast around for some excuse. "Not before they go!" She bowed her head toward Elias's teammates.

She was setting them up—Big Mike would go after them and probably the mafia's man too. But what choice did she have? They weren't taking her girls.

She'd already given up too many, let too many go without fighting for them. Not anymore.

Big Mike released her arm, but not without wrenching it as a reminder that he was bigger and stronger.

He underestimated her, though. Because she was angrier.

Behind the bar, her father always kept a loaded shotgun in case of trouble. He hadn't used it to get himself out of his situation with the Bratva, but she didn't have such reservations.

In a dead run, she zipped across the bar just as the special operatives headed toward Big Mike and the other guy. Four chests puffed out, they widened their stances, prepared to throw down and fight.

But she whipped out the shotgun, flipped the safety and blasted a hole directly through the glass door.

The mafia's man hit the deck. Just as she thought — he was all show and no substance. But Big Mike ignored her and took off for the stairs. The sound of his heavy thumping steps filled her with more of that burning smoke of anger. She could nearly taste its acridity in the base of her throat.

She tore after him, shotgun in hand.

"Ruby, stop!" The command came from the dark-eyed special operative. God, why didn't she know any of their names? Elias...Gasper...Jack...whoever he was, he had far too many, and they probably did too.

She didn't heed him — why should she? She plowed toward the stairs after Big Mike. She didn't make it five steps before an arm banded around her middle and yanked her down again. The weapon lifted from her hand.

"Gasper will rip off my balls if I let anything happen to you. I'll handle Mikhail."

Her stomach bottomed out at the mention of Elias. Where was he and how was her father? Were they both safe? When would she see them again?

She watched Elias's teammate run the stairs as if they were a flat surface. A few bumping noises later and a female shriek sounded. Ruby's eyes widened as her bouncer rolled head over heels down the stairs with a knot of women hot after him.

They were beating him in the face and kicking him in any body part they got access to. Several were screaming obscenities in Russian.

More women flooded into the restaurant, and the mafia's man raised his voice above all theirs and ordered them to the back door and into his truck.

At which point every girl in the room turned on him.

Ruby ran with them to attack. The wild looks on the women's faces made her believe that the special operative told them what their true destination was — and they were fighting back.

They wouldn't let that happen to them, and neither would Ruby. She caught the man's arm and used all her weight to pin it behind him while the girl next to her pulled his hair. Snippets of their cries rose up in a loud clamor, but she heard the door crash inward.

She twisted, wishing she had her shotgun to guard them against whoever was busting in, but as soon as her eyes landed on the man standing there, her heart gave a hard heave.

Elias covered the space between them in a blink. She started to turn to him, but he threw himself over her just as several gunshots came from the rear of the building.

A scream collected in her throat. "My girls!"

"Stay down."

Steel flashed as he whipped out a weapon and fired a shot. All the girls hit the floor, flattened and screaming or shaking where they stood, too stunned to move.

"Get down!" Ruby tried to scrabble free to force those frozen to the floor, but Elias hovered over her like a grizzly protecting a cub. She peeked around his muscled arm to see the room flooded with men that must be the Russian mafia. And determined to drive them out, the special ops team formed a massive wall. Each toted a high-powered rifle, and they weren't holding back.

Her toes dragged across the floor, and she realized Elias was bodily moving her. "I can't leave my girls! Don't you understand —"

His dark gaze hit hers like a physical blow. "Ruby — I can't lose you. Do as I say!"

"Well, you're not saying anything! You're just shoving me!"

With nothing more than a grunt in return, he shoved her again, moving her across the floor to a corner. She dragged in a deep breath and caught his wholesome scent. Like a whiff of spring rain, she wanted more. She clutched at his shirt and buried her face against his hard spine as he shielded her from what was happening in her restaurant.

An all-out war between his team and the men who'd ruled over her life this past year.

A couple girls broke free of the group and made a beeline for the stairs. She struggled toward them, but there was no moving past Elias. He was a steel cage she couldn't break free of.

When she tried to move again, he threw out an arm. "Stay put, woman!"

The harsh growl shouldn't turn her on, nor should him calling her "woman." But damn if a little thrill didn't move through her body.

When she took another peek around his arm, she saw why her mind was numbing itself to the actual battle in her restaurant. Glass shattered. Table legs were sheared off by bullets. Bodies fell to litter the floor and blood ran in streams. She pinched her eyes shut, hid behind Elias and waited for it all to end.

Her ears rang from the blasts, but it took her long minutes to realize it was totally silent. Her hands ached from gripping Elias's shirt so hard. She realized it, unfolding her stiff fingers.

"How many of my girls are dead?" she whispered, her throat dry. "How many?"

"Zero casualties among your girls." Elias couldn't be seeing things straight—there was too much blood. Every last girl under her care must have been wiped out.

"Don't lie to me!" she cried in a rough whisper that splintered.

He swung his weapon to the side and twisted to take her in his arms. Pulling her across into his arms, he smoothed the damp hair from her cheeks. She tried to turn her head and look at the scene, but he stopped her by cupping her cheek.

"Don't look. I'm getting you out of here now. Close your eyes."

She shook her head. "I can't leave. My girls!"

"My team's moving them out now."

Her throat closed. "They're not dead?"

His eyes burned with the truth. "Not a one."

Relief made her muscles slacken. She sagged against him, and next thing she knew, he was carrying her. She started to open her eyes, and he said, "Don't open them, Ruby. Believe me, you don't want to see."

Her stomach pitched and heaved like a tiny toy boat on the Bering Sea, but she didn't open her eyes. When fresh air hit her face, she gulped in a deep breath that staved off some of the nausea she felt.

"You can open them."

She slowly peeled her eyelids open and looked up into his ruggedly handsome face. "Usually when you're told to open your eyes, there's a surprise."

His lips quirked. "Surprise — a hot man is holding you."

In total opposition to all she was feeling, a laugh burst from her, unexpected and freeing.

She threw her arms around his neck. "Can the hot man kiss me or is he on duty?"

"I can sidestep the rules just this once."

She zeroed in on his full, hard lips, her body coming alive with each increment he lowered his mouth to hers. When his mouth crushed down, she sucked in a gasp and threw herself into the kiss.

Need and passion stole through her like rays of sunshine on a dark day. She parted her lips on a groan, and their tongues tangled in a dance her body needed to mimic.

The kiss lasted too brief a time, and Elias pulled away. She threaded her fingers into his thick hair and held him in place.

"I love you too. I'm probably too late to say it, but…"

He closed his eyes, his chest giving a heave. When he opened his eyes again, the depths were a blaze of love.

"It'll never be too late for us, sweetheart. Love doesn't work that way."

"Then you…still feel something…for me?"

He dropped his forehead to hers. "I'll never stop. You're it for me. I knew it when I set eyes on you."

A shiver of emotion coursed through her, and she snuggled closer in his arms. "Thank you for saving me."

"That's what Disney princes do."

She giggled. "I said our names sound as if we're twins."

"There's nothing familial about this, sweetheart."
He swooped in and captured her lips again, stealing
all thoughts.

All but one.

He hadn't told her yet, but she was free.

Gasper brushed his lips across Ruby's pert nipple.
When she gave him the soft moan he wanted from
her, he parted his lips around the bud and drew it
into his mouth.

She cried out, arching off the hotel bed. "Elias!"

He rumbled in answer and grazed the sensitive
bud with his teeth before lapping it with his tongue to
soothe the sharp pain.

Her breaths came in harsh pants. Her red waves
tumbled across the crisp white sheets, and her pale
skin was quickly growing pink from his
ministrations.

Every lick, nibble and suck he delivered to her
body had his cock throbbing harder and growing
steelier. The head was purple and shiny with precum.

"Don't stop!" she burst out when he slowed his
tongue.

Grinning, he raised his head to look into her eyes.
Taking his torment up a notch, he gained his knees
and closed his fist around the base of his cock. Her
stare latched on his hand while he gave it a slow jack.

Juice squeezed from the tip. Ruby licked her lips, and he damn near lost it. He was determined that this time — their fourth round of the night — he would remain in the driver's seat. But a single flick of her tongue across her sweet lips was driving him mad.

"Just one taste," she whispered.

"No."

"Please."

"Not a chance, beautiful. This time you're going to be the one screaming down the rafters." To prove his point, he dragged two fingers down the seam of her breasts, all the way to her navel. Her stomach dipped in on a gasp when he crested over her mound and pressed down on her clit.

"Let me...suck your cock," she cried out.

"No."

"But..."

He shoved her thighs apart and shouldered his way between them. When he parted her damp lips with his thumbs and saw how wet she was, he growled. "Not. A. Chance."

He speared her with his tongue. Splitting her slick folds, burrowing deep, deeper, questing to give her the biggest orgasm of her life. One that would steal any belief she could walk away from him after this.

Or walk straight.

Hell, walk at all.

He stroked his tongue up her seam to crush over her clit. She gulped and writhed. After keeping her in this bed with him, he knew her trigger points, and no way would he let up until she was screaming his name.

The flush on her skin and the small cries escaping her bitten lips had his cock pounding harder. If he stared at her lips too long, he'd give in and let her suck his cock, but that ended too fast with her at the wheel.

Slipping two fingers into her tight sheath, he pulled the first pulsation from her. Her inner walls squeezed. Then clamped down. She stopped breathing as she teetered on the brink. He held her there for long moments and then finally pulsed his fingers in and out of her fast.

Her hips jerked off the bed, and she called out his name. Christ, watching her face as she came apart for him was his new secret obsession. He couldn't get enough—would never get enough.

He'd marry this woman if she agreed to it. Problem was, she hadn't agreed to return to the base with him or even to live in the nearest village to be close to him.

She claimed she loved him, and her body told him as much. So why was she holding back?

A last cry burst from her lips. She collapsed to the bed, knees splayed while he slowly lapped her pussy clean of juices and lost more of his heart to her.

251

When he raised his head and met her stare, the words rushed out. "Marry me."

She stared.

Feeling this was right to the marrow of his bones, he crawled up her body to hover over her, braced on his arms. His erection jutted against her pussy. A small shove and he'd be inside that slick heat he craved. But not yet.

"I mean it, Ruby. Marry me. Let me make you my life. I can't imagine living any other way."

She didn't speak, and he went on, "I want to keep you safe. Make you happy. Give you everything you've never had."

She stopped him with a finger over his lips. Still, she didn't speak. At last, she shook her head. "Don't you know you give me all those things? I never believed I'd have a man like you. The men I've seen were horrible or selfish. My own father was so selfish he trapped me in his hell."

Her father was being released from the hospital soon, after a long course of treatment for malnutrition and infection and a surgery to fix what they could of his fingers. When he was ready, he said he wanted to return to Ruby's Place and run it the way his mother meant for it to be run, minus the brothel. Though Elias had questions about his ability to stay out of trouble when it came to gambling, he hoped the man proved honest from here forward.

And left his daughter out of it.

Ruby brushed her fingertips over his lips and trailed them across his jaw. She searched his eyes. "You've given me my life back."

"You can choose what you want to do with it. Don't you see that?"

Her mouth popped open as if what he said finally hit home.

Seeing he'd struck a nerve, and maybe could convince her to say yes, he stared down at her. "You don't actually believe you deserve your life back, do you?"

She didn't speak. She pushed against his chest, and he rolled off her, still hard and throbbing, but sex was far from his thoughts. When she sat on the side of the bed, he stood up and circled to kneel in front of her. He took her hand and squeezed her fingers.

"Ruby, you're deserving."

She looked away. "I didn't always choose the correct path. I screwed up."

"Nobody's perfect. You were in a desperate situation."

"But I sent girls away to fend for themselves."

"The world needs rules to keep operating. I employ those rules to keep people safe, and you did the same."

She dropped her stare to their joined hands. "When my girls were in the middle of that gun fight, I knew I'd failed them."

He set his fingertip beneath her chin and drew her eyes up to meet his. "Sweetheart, you never failed. You couldn't have stopped the mafia from rushing in there. They opened fire on us because they knew we were about to end their reign."

When a shiver ran through her, he wrapped her in a blanket, stood and drew her into his lap. She curled against him, which gave his heart a pang of love mingled with pain.

"I was self-centered. Focused on saving my father. I should have been less selfish."

"Let's say for a second that you were selfish — that you could have done more. Then let me ask you if you'd do it all the same way."

She shook her head before he finished the sentence.

"See?" He hugged her closer, breathing in her sweet scent. "You changed. Grew. That's what life is."

"How do you know all this?"

He shrugged. "They call me the jack-of-all-trades for a reason."

She arched a brow. "I've been wondering about that. What's the reason?"

"I'm not one to talk myself up, but I only need to see something once to learn how to do it."

"I don't understand."

"I saw how you selflessly gave up everything in order to keep your father alive. You love with no restrictions — and you taught me to do the same."

She made a hitching noise in her chest, and he drew her chin up to meet her eyes again.

"Say yes, Ruby. Say you'll be my wife."

A tear zigzagged down her cheek, and he caught it with his thumb. Then, as if the sun broke through the clouds, a smile lit up her face. A soft laugh bubbled past her lips.

"Yes." She leaned into his palm. "I'll marry you."

He stared at her. "Really?"

"Yes!"

He bracketed her face in his hands and kissed her. The passion flowed between them, growing stronger with promise of their yet-to-be-spoken vows.

Then she pushed on his chest, sending him sprawling on the bed. She straddled him and threw off the blanket he'd cloaked her in.

Planting his hands on her curvy hips, he drew her onto his cock. In a hard thrust, she took his length to the hilt. Need blasted up from his balls and tightened around every inch of his erection inside her. She moaned, and he claimed it with his tongue swirling over hers.

She rocked on him, again and again, pulling his hard cock through her slippery hot sheath. When he felt her begin to tighten on him, he locked her body close to his and rocked his hips to fuck her.

Love shattered his heart at the moment she began to come. A spurt burst from him, and he roared with the ecstasy taking over his body.

His heart. His soul.

Ruby undulated her hips a final time, trying to kill him. He grunted and rolled, pinning her beneath him again.

"You sure you love me?" he rasped.

Confusion lit her stormy blue-gray eyes. "Why would you ask me that? I just told you I'll marry you."

He offered her a sly glance. "Well, I may have jumped the gun and made some plans."

"What kind of plans?" Outrage sounded in her tone.

"I rented us a place. It's a shack really, but I'm handy."

"Don't tell me you know how to build too."

"I'm skilled with a hammer and saw."

"You got a house for us before knowing I'd say yes?"

He searched her beautiful eyes. "It's called hope, sweetheart. I hoped and prayed that you'd be at my side for the rest of my life."

She shoved him in the chest. "You mean you knew you'd get your way."

He grinned down at her. "I have an edge, you must admit."

"What's that? Being cocky enough to believe everything will go in your favor?"

He chuckled and twisted a lock of her hair around his finger. "I have enough sex positions to keep you satisfied for a lifetime stored up here." He tapped a fingertip to his temple." Besides, I haven't showed you how fun that washing machine can really be."

Lust flooded her eyes again. "Maybe you'd better show me some of those positions now. The washer will have to wait."

He cocked a brow. "How many times do you want to come tonight?"

She locked her thighs around his hips. "Why don't you show me what you're made of, baby?"

"Mmm. That's a name I haven't been called yet."

"Gasper. Elias. Jack. Doesn't matter what they call you." She kissed him with a tender brush of her lips and then whispered, "You're all mine."

"I knew I'd win you someday. Quitters never win." He twitched his hips, filling her with his cock again and listening to her soft cries grow louder until a final scream issued from her. Seconds after his final jet of cum left him, a loud banging shattered through his haze of pleasure.

"Dammit, I'm gonna kill these guys if it's not important." He yanked on his jeans while Ruby rolled up like a burrito in the covers to conceal her nakedness.

He strode to the hotel room door and unchained it. One peek through the peephole showed him the fisheye view of Penn standing there. When Gasper opened the door, all the guys burst out laughing.

"You guys are damn loud, ya know that?" Shadow ribbed him.

Gasper shot a glance over his shoulder at the bed. Ruby pulled the covers over her head to hide her blush.

"What do you assholes want?" He grinned at his brothers.

"We're celebrating. Meet us in the bar. Both of you." Penn shot a glance past him toward Ruby.

Gasper scratched his head. "What's to celebrate?"

"Paxton made it through his second surgery, and they say he'll be good as new and joining us as soon as he finishes rehab." Penn's words brought a rousing cheer from the rest of the team.

Gasper grinned. "Damn, that is good news. Give us five minutes. We'll meet you."

After he was finished and Ruby poked her head out from beneath the covers, they shared a smile. "Such good news."

He walked over to the bed and slapped her bare ass as she climbed out of bed to dress. She squealed, and he barely held his need in check as they dressed. He grabbed her hand and threaded their fingers together.

Tenderness and pure love filled him. For another today in his life. For his brothers. Paxton.

For Ruby.

To his surprise, she went on tiptoe and pecked him on the cheek.

"What's that for?" he asked.

"We have some good news of our own to share, don't we? Let's go. I could use a drink that I don't have to serve for once." She tugged his hand, drawing him faster down the hallway to the bar. He'd follow the strong woman who was the love of his life anywhere.

1-CLICK THE NEXT IN SERIES
Paxton's story
XTREME PRESSURE

Time is running out.
It also has a way of showing you
what really matters...

Em Petrova

Em Petrova was raised by hippies in the wilds of Pennsylvania but told her parents at the age of four she wanted to be a gypsy when she grew up. She has a soft spot for babies, puppies and 90s Grunge music and believes in Bigfoot and aliens. She started writing at the age of twelve and prides herself on making her characters larger than life and her sex scenes hotter than hot.

She burst into the world of publishing in 2010 after having five beautiful bambinos and figuring they were old enough to get their own snacks while she pounds away at the keys. In her not-so-spare time, she is fur-mommy to a Labradoodle named Daisy Hasselhoff.

Find More Books by Em Petrova at empetrova.com

Other Titles by Em Petrova

West Protection
RESCUED BY THE COWBOY

GUARDED BY THE COWBOY
COWBOY CONSPIRACY THEORY
COWBOY IN THE CORSSHAIRS
PROTECTED BY THE COWBOY

Xtreme Ops
HITTING XTREMES
TO THE XTREME
XTREME BEHAVIOR
XTREME AFFAIRS
XTREME MEASURES
XTREME PRESSURE
XTREME LIMITS
Xtreme Ops Alaska Search and Rescue
NORTH OF LOVE

Crossroads
BAD IN BOOTS
CONFIDENT IN CHAPS
COCKY IN A COWBOY HAT
SAVAGE IN A STETSON
SHOW-OFF IN SPURS

Dark Falcons MC
DIXON

TANK
PATRIOT
DIESEL
BLADE

The Guard
HIS TO SHELTER
HIS TO DEFEND
HIS TO PROTECT

Moon Ranch
TOUGH AND TAMED
SCREWED AND SATISFIED
CHISELED AND CLAIMED

Ranger Ops
AT CLOSE RANGE
WITHIN RANGE
POINT BLANK RANGE
RANGE OF MOTION
TARGET IN RANGE
OUT OF RANGE

Knight Ops Series
ALL KNIGHTER
HEAT OF THE KNIGHT

HOT LOUISIANA KNIGHT
AFTER MIDKNIGHT
KNIGHT SHIFT
ANGEL OF THE KNIGHT
O CHRISTMAS KNIGHT

Wild West Series
SOMETHING ABOUT A LAWMAN
SOMETHING ABOUT A SHERIFF
SOMETHING ABOUT A BOUNTY HUNTER
SOMETHING ABOUT A MOUNTAIN MAN

Operation Cowboy Series
KICKIN' UP DUST
SPURS AND SURRENDER

The Boot Knockers Ranch Series
PUSHIN' BUTTONS
BODY LANGUAGE
REINING MEN
ROPIN' HEARTS
ROPE BURN
COWBOY NOT INCLUDED
COWBOY BY CANDLELIGHT
THE BOOT KNOCKER'S BABY
ROPIN' A ROMEO

COWBOY CRUSHIN' Witt's story
COWBOY SECRET Beck's story
COWBOY RUSH Kade's Story
COWBOY MISTLETOE a Christmas novella
COWBOY FLIRTATION Ford's story
COWBOY TEMPTATION Easton's story
COWBOY SURPRISE Justus's story
COWGIRL DREAMER Gracie's story
COWGIRL MIRACLE Jessamine's story
COWGIRL HEART Kezziah's story

Single Titles and Boxes
THE BOOT KNOCKERS RANCH BOX SET
THE DALTON BOYS BOX SET
SINFUL HEARTS
JINGLE BOOTS
A COWBOY FOR CHRISTMAS
FULL RIDE

Club Ties Series
LOVE TIES
HEART TIES
MARKED AS HIS
SOUL TIES
ACE'S WILD

Firehouse 5 Series

ONE FIERY NIGHT

CONTROLLED BURN

SMOLDERING HEARTS

Hardworking Heroes Novellas

STRANDED AND STRADDLED

DALLAS NIGHTS

SLICK RIDER

SPURRED ON

EM PETROVA
WWW.EMPETROVA.COM